The
Tiller
of
Waters

The Tiller of Waters

Hoda Barakat

Translated by Marilyn Booth

The American University in Cairo Press
Cairo   New York

English translation copyright © 2001 by
The American University in Cairo Press
113 Sharia Kasr el Aini, Cairo, Egypt
420 Fifth Avenue, New York, NY 10018

First published in Arabic in 1998 as *Harith al-miyah*
Copyright © 1998 by Hoda Barakat
Protected under the Berne Convention

Dar el Kutub No.11880/01
ISBN 977 424 690 X

Designed by Andrea El-Akshar/AUC Press Design Center
Printed in Egypt

People make objects and construct houses, but it is emptiness alone that gives them meaning. Lack is what gives meaning to existence.
Lao Tsu

The notion of posterity is nothing but the sense of irrepressible revenge that hounds us . . . . These diverse stretches of time that we have lived are more dedicated to letters and names than they are to the parts of our bodies . . . .
Pascal Quignard

The Chinese philosopher Zhuangzi reported that in a dream he saw a little butterfly who gazed at him . . . and when he awoke, he asked himself: Am I now a dream-construction, a philosopher looking at a butterfly in the butterfly's dream?

The Prophet Muhammad said:
People are sleepers who awake when they die.

In a desolate region of Persia a stone tower was built, of modest height, without a door or window. In its singular chamber, round and paved with flagstones, were a wooden table and a chair. In this round room, a man who resembled me was hunched over the long poem that he was composing in letters I did not understand, about a man living in another circular chamber writing a poem about a man in another circular chamber . . .
There is no end to this path, and no one will ever come to read what the prisoners write.
Jorge Luis Borges

I chanted the purple of Tyre, our mother. I chanted the works of those who discovered the alphabet and tilled the waters. I chanted the burnt sacrifice of the renowned queen. I chanted the masts and oars . . . and the piercing agonies . . . .
Jorge Luis Borges, from a terracotta tablet, anonymously authored

I t's an illusion. It is only an illusion that you see, said my father to my mother, who stared into the distance, her hand raised to shade her eyes from the sun.

From such a distance, you cannot see what you claim to see. The sea is like the desert: it, too, has its own mirages. And we are still far from land.

But—I told your father—it was certainly Beirut. The ship carrying us from Alexandria to Greece, hugging the shoreline to escape the turbulence of the open sea's surging waves, was at this very moment sailing opposite Ras Beirut, which I really did see. From a distance, it looked so lovely. It looked like a landscape of dreams. I no longer felt the cravings of pregnancy, or the nausea brought on by the furious waves. For the first time in months, I longed once again to sing. As I pressed against the deck's metal railing, I raised my arms—so plump and white they were—to wave toward the shore, and said to your father, I want us to go ashore here. I don't want to go to Greece. And that is exactly what happened.

Yet, in all of my fifty years, not once have I believed my mother's version of the story. My father, always remaining silent, would simply look at her and smile, as though his love for her had left him fearful of casting the least doubt on her words. As if she were a delicately pretty blossom that the slightest affront would crush. But her many narratives, a trice different each time, left it to me to envision what scraps of truth might be behind my mother's tales.

I never asked her how it was—as she played the role of pregnant woman aboard the vessel transporting her, my father, and his Greek business partner to Salonica—that the sunshine could have been so brilliant if stormy waves were forcing the ship close to shore. Perhaps, I told myself, the storm had struck out at sea but the sun persisted in shining on its verges. I did not ask her if the land that so delighted her eyes could have been Cyprus, or perhaps Crete, rather than the land of her forefathers. I did not ask her how she was able through force of will and coquetry to turn the ship; how she guided it into Beirut harbor and got it to anchor, whereupon she disembarked with my father while his Greek partner went on to Greece. Everyone must have left the ship at Salonica, I told myself, and then at her insistence my father dissolved his partnership, took his share, and embarked again with my mother, this time for Beirut. There I was born and there I grew up, in the quarter of Abu Jmil. We stayed there until the war was three years old. There my father's business as a textile merchant blossomed, and when he died he had already turned over to me his spacious and well-known shop in Souq Tawile where I live now.

It was not father's death that made life with mother difficult; my life with her had always been so. I had defeated her expectations over and over. Being born a boy was the first disappointment. She had hoped for a girl who would replicate some of her own feminine good looks and thereby serve as testament to my mother's beauty. Until I reached puberty my mother persisted in teaching me the operatic singing for which she had spent her whole life preparing, all the while telling us of her erstwhile singing career. She never showed any disappointment, as far as I can judge, when she discovered that Beirut did not have the Opera House whose existence she had assumed, it seems, as long as she still lived in Cairo. Every time she went to her Armenian singing teacher—who had established a school near to the Lazarist Convent—she returned home full of delight, assuring us that the performance was imminent and Professor Kevork had entrusted her with the premier role. My father never challenged anything she said or did. He even took care that she didn't see him shaking salt surreptitiously over his plate after she had declared that the food was excellent just as it was (although *she* was not one to enter the kitchen and prepare a meal with her own hands). And then, my father would add salt to his food whenever, complaining, she added it to hers with her eyes steadily on him. Out of her hearing, a touch of wretchedness glimmering in his eyes, my father said to me: There are women of silk . . . your mother . . . she is a woman of silk. When you're older, you will understand.

When she decided that they would live in Beirut he did not object, despite all he had heard from his father, also a native of Beirut, who had talked to him at great length about that city and had read much of its lore to him. My grandfather would end their sessions by admonishing his son not to fall into the trap of Beirut's temptations, not to one day consider it his cherished destination just because it had once been the land of his ancestors. No, my father did not oppose my mother in anything at all, even when she dressed me in girls' clothes against my wishes, instructed me at home on how to sing opera, and took me along to the school of Professor Kevork with his pencil-thin Douglas Fairbanks moustaches. There, before leaving me in a gloomy corner while she went over to stand by the piano where Professor Kevork sat, she always charged me to open my ears and listen well. And before sleep could overcome me as I heard the same delicately echoing musical phrases over and over, I would sketch my mental picture of my mother's upper half, submerged now in darkness, and her pleasing mouth open in song. For the lamplight illuminated only her lower half and the moustaches of Professor Kevork, bent over the instrument.

I was a disappointment to her because as a child I was not a good singer, and then my voice started to thicken, becoming hoarse and unreliable. I lost my soprano register before I had even reached my twelfth year. Meanwhile, my mother grew completely convinced that I would never be a successful student either. I would never be any better off than my father, the trader in cloth . . . . And it was almost as if she capitulated to this particular disappointment when my father began to take me along to his shop. I came to spend all of my free days there. On our school half days, Wednesdays and Fridays, he always promised her that he would hear me learn my lessons and supervise my homework, making sure I would finish it in the shop. Her only response was to avert her face in a gesture of seeming despair. After we had eaten lunch he would tuck my leather briefcase under his arm and wave my mother off to her singing practice. Now I would not be in the house to disturb her.

4   Sometimes we stayed late in the shop. When that happened, before my father charged his senior shop assistant to lock up, before he wished his cronies goodnight, he would say to me under his breath: We are a disgrace! Your mother must be hungry by now; we weren't watching the time. That was the line that always told me I would soon be shrouded in a cumbersome bouquet of roses whose thorns would poke into my hands, or flowers whose enormous leaves would prevent me from seeing the lights of the city as we made our way home. First, though, my father would make one of his usual detours, stopping at the Souq des Francs to buy some nice-looking fruit, or in Bab Idris at his friend Rifai's little shop, where he would buy roasted pistachios that were still hot. Only then did we hurry home, rushing down Rue Ahmed al-Daouk and turning onto our own street. If we could not hear the wail of my mother's gramophone as we climbed the stairs, my father would start preparing a long and elaborate excuse. He might rap lightly on the glass pane set into the door of our chatty neighbor Sarah's apartment, and if she appeared to be alone he would ask her to come up and spend the evening with us. Sarah knew exactly what was going on, and she would give her head a

complicitous nod. Listening to Sarah's mischievous gossip, my mother would stop thinking about her own irritation and the evening would unfold reasonably well.

None of these ploys worked, though, when my father's conversation with his merchant friends delved into politics or became submerged in the world of textiles. On those evenings, as we left the shop we would turn left from the market street. We would walk a short way down Rue Weygand to La Damascène, where my father would pause, bemused. Which out-of-season fruits should he choose for my mother, paying the sort of exorbitant price shelled out by those shy, embarrassed men who, at the behest of their pampered, pregnant wives, request grapes in the winter month of Shubat or perhaps a ripe, red watermelon?

That is why, after my father's death, I found it so difficult to keep my mother contented. It was not only that I had abandoned my studies and so betrayed her dreams that I would become a physician, a scholar of music, or the like, but also that, in the fabric business, I would never fill my father's shoes. I would never acquire his finest qualities, she believed, never equal his ample abilities. And she was more or less right about that. When I began to work regularly in the store, at his side, I could not imagine myself alone behind the counter, without him. I always envisioned us together, the two of us as sole proprietor—one and the same. But my mother, who saw me as future heir to the business, could not be persuaded of my worth by the modest aptitude I did possess, not even by my merit as a mere shop assistant to my father who would not live on and on until the end of my life simply for my sake.

Even as a little boy I had tried very hard to figure out how it was that my father seemed always to understand my mother. It became far more difficult after his death, for I lost the exemplar I had had before me and she lost her already meager desire to express herself, to make any gesture at all that would tell me what she wanted.

Even so, much of the time she repeated a single phrase: He sees noth-

5

ing . . . he sees nothing but what he wants to see. She would go on and on in that vein, as if still talking to her sister, as if her sister were still there in the parlor and had not left us long before. My mother's voice was always low; she spoke in a monotone, every breath controlled, every sequence of sounds balanced and even. She did not react visibly to anything. She did not raise her voice in anger; she never softened it in a whispered confidence. Her voice never detached itself from her face, never sailed across the windowsill like those maternal voices that did reach my ears from outside. If you did not look at my mother directly, you would not hear her when she spoke. If you did hear her, you would not understand what she was saying unless you were gazing full into her face.

Of course she must have been right. He sees nothing but what he wants to see. As a little boy, when I heard her call out to me I would not turn directly to her. I would stare more or less in the direction of her face but focus elsewhere as I listened to her voice. Her sister told her repeatedly that it was a habit of shy people; they avoid looking directly into the eyes of those who are speaking to them. No, my mother would answer. It is the habit of the blind.

Yes, my mother's voice was invariably low, calm, and smooth. And after the death of my father I altered my habits. I worked to imitate him. I looked straight at her, watching her expression closely to grasp what she meant and to make out what she wanted. I was all she had now, and she had grown old. Yet, faced with the unabated persistence with which she rationed her voice, I began to convince myself that she really was trying to preserve and take care of it. It was not a mere malevolent desire to refuse contact with whoever tried to speak to her, making him work extremely hard to surmount the difficulties of understanding what she might want.

For until the very last years of her life my mother insisted that her voice was the most beautiful of female voices to ever exist. She never quit training it, priming herself for that operatic debut. But at the point when her preparations became truly elaborate, accompanied by her changeable narratives as she took up her cosmetic pencil to redraw the lineaments of her face, I was seized with a terrible anxiety for her. Surely, I thought, my mother was growing feeble-minded with age. But I soon began listening to her stories differently, questioning myself, skeptical of my own presuppositions. After all, had there ever been a time when my mother dwelt in reality? Had anyone ever been able to claim that in her youth she had told only the truth? Who could say that her tales, as variable as they were now in her old age, were not for the most part true, that they did not record events that had actually taken place? Armed with powder and cosmetic tools, she redrew the lines of her face when age had erased her features, for she could not endure that effacement. I would come back from the shop in the evening to find her sitting on her chaise longue. She would have started her story before I could even appear. Washing my hands, I would carry the dinner tray already prepared by Shamsa into my mother's room and would sit down opposite her. Staring at her red hair, at the fine eyebrows drawn by black pencil in the shape of arched twin bridges, I would listen.

I sang at the King's birthday celebration. Queen Nazli had pleaded with me for such a long time! That was where your grandfather caught sight of me and was enchanted. Your grandfather . . . in defiance of him and of cloth, I carried his son off to Beirut. He was besotted, but he hated me, too. He was afraid of me, afraid of my voice. He feared that I would become an artiste, a famous one, because I was so beautiful and my voice was sublime. He moved mountains to keep me from ever singing again for the King. If I were to return to the palace, he told his son, Farouk would surely add me to his harem. And what shame it would bring down on him if he were to marry me after that! But then, after opposing it for so long, he made hasty arrangements with my father for my marriage.

As my mother spoke of these things, her voice fell back into the rhythms of the Egyptian dialect.

I carried your father off to Beirut, a provocation to his father because he detested this city, though I could not keep your father away from fabrics as I had dreamed of doing. Even a few days before we traveled, your grandfather was still telling him how grand a country Greece was, and warning your father against settling down in Beirut, for he had an inkling of my wishes . . . . The city is heading toward earthquake, he said; I was told so by the Englishman, the professor from Leeds University. Affecting a scientific objectivity, your grandfather would say that Beirut sat atop a fault that slipped five millimeters each year. According to current geological research, he would say, that was a major rift. And earthquakes turned everything bottom-side up—that's what he would say. Quakes had twice wiped the city off the earth already, and there was no doubt that the third convulsion was due. The time has come for the third, he would say, and we're not even counting the havoc of wars . . . .

This city is no one's country, my father would say when angry, replicating the words of my grandfather. And more often than not in the final years of his life, my father was angry. He despaired over what he called the era of synthetic fabrics—the Age of Diolen, he would say; and the Age of Diolen, he lamented, had left him—and now me—with too much spare time in which to converse. Retail movement had dwindled to the point where we needed to keep on only a single shop assistant. My father's eyes as he gazed at me held a flicker of sadness, or perhaps it was pity. And then he would say that his father had probably been right.

In the last years of his life he summoned back his father's words for hours at a time. It seemed as though he wanted to command his father's presence in our conversations, to fetch my grandfather for his grandson in an era of such singular stinginess that it compelled one to dwell on the riches of the past. It seemed as though my father wanted to prod me to forget how miserable were the present fortunes of fabric by returning me

to the prosperity of his absent father—the wealth of all that had surrounded him, and the wealth of his golden words, as it pleased my father
to say when overcome by his yearning for that past.

But now I live in a state of happiness and ease that my father and
mother could not have imagined during their lives. How could they have
ever envisioned what has befallen my days and the life of our city? For
these are things that no one could have foreseen. I live now as I always
hoped to live. Nothing disturbs my equilibrium. It is as if all of our longings, our aspirations—my grandfather's, my father's, and mine, and perhaps even my mother's—have come to fruition, embodied in my present
life. The past calls out only to those, like my father, who have been
deceived by their present. Yet I find myself slipping sometimes into his
tender nostalgia, for all along I saw him more as twin brother than as
father. What is more, for me as for my mother he stands for qualities that
I never could locate in myself, especially after he died and I lost all hope
of learning from him, of acquiring his talents at his own hand . . . and
after the life I live now endowed me with time and leisure such that I
could review the lessons I learned from him, which took the place in my
head of the lessons I learned in school, only a few traces of which have
remained with me.

I see now what I truly want to see. The city did not betray me as my grandfather feared it would. This was the grandfather for whom my father had named me, even though my mother went on calling me Daoud, alluding to my stubbornness, reducing to two syllables the popular expression that she had made her refrain: To whom are you reciting your psalms?

Hurry, Hajj Niqula, said Abd al-Karim, son of Abu Abd al-Karim, whose shop was a mere few meters' distance from ours. I took my seat next to him in his Honda, while the six-wheel truck we had rented, splitting the cost evenly, followed. The truck could not penetrate the souq from Rue Weygand. Not only was the way into the market too narrow to bear the trailer but also the narrow lanes there were crammed with merchants' vans, small pickup trucks, and crowds of people hurrying in every direction, shouting and making such a commotion that no one could hear anyone else. Abd al-Karim motioned to the truck driver to turn from Rue al-Houaik into Rue de Tripoli. From there he should try to enter the souq, pushing forward as far as he could toward our shops, which in any case were located in the section of the souq down toward the sea.

We had not yet reached our shops when I remarked to Abd al-Karim that people were crazy. It was perfectly calm and clear out and there was no need for such hysteria. Hush, Hajj, said Abd al-Karim. Your Lord protect us—I just hope that what we find to bring out is enough to cover the cost of renting that truck.

Abd al-Karim stopped his Honda at the corner of Rue Khan Fakhri Bek; the crowd was too dense to go any further. As the porters who had come with the truck followed us on foot, he said: Let's take care of my family's shop first since it's closer to the truck. Hurrying after him, I agreed.

We were still several meters from his father's shop when we heard explosions nearby. Abd al-Karim paid no attention as he plodded on, but when he reached the shop entrance he came to an abrupt stop. The sliding steel door was distended outward like a ball and the bars were badly gashed. Praise God! I was fearing the worst, Abd al-Karim said. But there's been no fire here.

Once inside the shop, Abd al-Karim seemed oblivious to the quantities of ruined merchandise. Some rolls of fabric were in shreds and more lay in heaps on the floor and the wooden counter. He left the shop in search of our porters but found no one.

We returned to Abd al-Karim's car. As its wheels devoured the asphalt, his insults and curses cascaded out. Abd al-Karim measured them out on the Kurds and their ilk, by whom he meant the porters and the truck driver, who had all disappeared in a flash after the strafing intensified, without informing us. They had been paid in advance, availing themselves of the 'circumstances' to insist that we meet every one of their conditions. As we sat in the house sipping coffee, Abd al-Karim insisted that the goods plundered from the souq were even now being unloaded from the trucks in Jummaize and Ashrafiye. They steal from us, he said angrily, and then they bomb us to keep us from rescuing our goods. It's all planned in advance, everything is calculated; this is a war for plunder. It is not a war of men. This is a conspiracy, a diabolic plot. You will find all of their shops empty, and ours are torched once they've been plundered. You know me, Hajj Niqula, and your father knows my father. Are we fanatics? Have you caught a whiff of fanaticism in us anything like the sort those people are showing?

Abd al-Karim felt no embarrassment about alluding to the Maronites in this manner. He knew that we—the Greek Orthodox—did not like them very much either. He knew that we had no part in what was happening and nothing to do with those whom he called foreign imports imposed on the native Beirutis. He was even under the impression that I had been thinking of putting myself forward to request the hand of his maternal cousin, daughter of his uncle Muhyi al-Din, so much did I stumble over my words when she came by their shop one day with a girlfriend of hers while I happened to be there. I had already seen her in our shop. She had come in with Abd al-Karim one time to see if we still had any atlaz, the satiny, rose-colored bedlinen fabric for which she was searching. It was one of the fabrics that my father had hesitated long about, but then had reluctantly set out in the front of our shop. He called it "the upholsterers' stuff," and he never hurried to bring it inside the shop when the rain came down. It's only atlaz, he would say. Not atlas, which is true silk. Pay attention, Niqula.

Abd al-Karim had no doubts that my stuttering, when I saw her the second time, was a reaction to the way his father glowered and the man's suddenly arid tone when he addressed me. It was a startling change, meant to tell me clearly that Abd al-Karim's cousin was further from my grasp than were the stars in the heavens.

What will I say to my father the Hajj now? Abd al-Karim was saying over and over, his air desolate, shaking my hand as we parted at my door. We will come back soon, Abd al-Karim, when the situation calms down, I assured him. I had not yet seen our shop, I told him, not even from a distance.

It was true. I had not even gone to look at our shop, not even caught a distant glimpse of it. I did not share Abd al-Karim's tense gloom. I felt guilty about my indifference, which prevailed even after the fighting intensified in the city center and there was a meeting of the leading souq merchants in the home of one of them in the quarter of Musaitbe. Everyone assured everyone else that whatever had not been destroyed by fire had been rifled. The meeting concluded with the formation of a committee of merchants. But I never returned to meet with them. Why, I would ask myself, was my heart so cold? I know that in one manner or another, and because I had not seen it with my own eyes, I was holding on to the hope that our shop had remained unharmed. But the real reason was otherwise. It lay in my aberrant nature, in things about myself that astonished even me, things that I could not but recognize when my father died.

For when the doctor, closing the door to the room behind him, told me that my father had given up his soul, my heart did not shatter from grief as I had anticipated and imagined many times, standing beside my father's sickbed or shut in my room crying out my pain at his impending death. I even considered asking the doctor whether Jirjis Mitri had really and truly died. It seemed as if I had become two people, one urging the other to show grief—even if it were a sham—when in front of people or with my mother, while the other person remained vacant, idle, empty of all feeling . . . . It seemed as if my father had also become two people. One of them was indeed my father, and the other was that Jirjis Mitri who had just died. His pain has burned up his tears, some people said. It is how they chose to explain why I showed none of the usual physical signs of mourning.

When my mother died it was different. I accompanied her body in the parish car to the cemetery at Mar Mitr. No one was there but the priest, the sacristan, and a few members of the parish whom I did not know personally. I felt no embarrassment about my failure to weep. And when I refused to stay the night with one of the parishioners, the priest urged me to return quickly to my own home, catching a ride with the hearse driver. Hearses were not stopped at the roadblocks that dotted the roads between Ashrafiye and Starco.

That is the way it is with me sometimes. I can be walking along next to my own body as if I am observing it. I won't feel that what has happened to me is real until after considerable time has passed.

The first time that it even occurred to me to go and inspect the shop, I had been staying for more than two months on Rue Graham with Hanoun, who had insisted on it so strongly that I could not get away. That was more than two years after the day on which I had gone into the souq with Abd al-Karim.

Hanoun appeared on a Sunday afternoon, as he had always used to do. He swallowed his coffee, took his crochet hooks from his bag, and began to work the wool and chat as if the city were not in the midst of a war, as if he had not stopped visiting after my father had clearly and unequivocally let him know that his presence in our house was not welcome. It was not Hanoun's tendency to chatter on and on that bothered my father. It was not those long fingers that flashed gold rings as he crocheted his yarn, nor was it my father's disgust at the way he attached himself to my mother so devotedly, nor his flimsy gestures, so like those of pampered women and cinema actresses . . . . No. The reason was that Hanoun's two sisters worked in the cabarets, under assumed names and blond wigs. When my father told him one day that he was not a man, Hanoun responded in annoyance. You have an outdated mentality, he spluttered. You're one of those people who still consider it shameful to be an artist.

Artist! Go artist yourself, responded my father. Do you really believe that people don't know that 'Flora' and 'Dolly' are your sisters Afifa and Latifa? Everyone knows they are belly dancers in a cabaret in Zaytouna.

Singers! Hanoun corrected him, as he caught in midair the bowl of roasted chestnuts my father had hurled at him. And he added, almost weeping, I swear, they are singers! Ask Tante, she knows. He was pointing to my mother. She's heard Flora's lovely voice, God keep her safe for my sake.

The end of Hanoun's plaint was heard only by the steps as he ran down the staircase, his high voice swearing by the coarsest of oaths that he would not return to that house as long as he lived, in spite of his great love for me and for my mother. For then perhaps my father would see for himself how very much in error he had been and how much he had wronged Hanoun.

Even after my father died, Hanoun did not resume his weekly visits. So I was completely unprepared when he rapped on my door on this particular Sunday afternoon. He had come, he insisted, consumed by worry. He longed to reassure himself that we were safe and to hear how we were getting along. When he learned that my mother had died, he sobbed. He told me that his sisters had traveled to Alexandria shortly after the 'events' began. He had stayed on to guard the house but was soon to join them.

Hanoun wandered through every room in our house, repeating that it was too high, too exposed, and too close to the shelling and the battles that were tearing apart the city center. Then he rummaged about for a suitcase. Pulling one out, he invited me to collect my things—because, he said, he certainly was not going to leave me in this house by myself while he stayed alone at home, secure in Rue Graham. He picked up the suitcase and instructed me to make sure the gas was shut off before striding out of the apartment to precede me down the stairs at nearly a run.

Sitting across from him in his own living room as he kept up a commentary on politics, I became aware of how much Hanoun had aged and how thin he had gotten. It had never been his wont to talk politics. His hands fluttered in the same familiar gestures, as if he were still chattering to my mother about women's affairs, as my father would have said. Wanting to make a point of his incredulity, time and again he smacked his palms against his thighs, jerking his head dramatically to the right while rolling his eyes. Throughout the days I spent at his home, he went on and on explaining to me how and why he had decided to become a communist, considering that he had been slow to do so in comparison to his sisters, who had long understood that the Orthodox must all become communists because our Mother Russia was communist. You know, those two girls whose art your father mocked? They were communists in fact as well as in name, plain and simple, not like me, talking to you now as I sit here comfortably on a sofa. I didn't say as much to your father because he hated communists even more than he did art and artists.

Why, I asked Hanoun, did he not go straight over to the Communist Party headquarters and defend his convictions publicly as they did, and fight at their side? He was old now, he responded, and no longer of any use for anything. He kept up his ideas for his own sake, and in anticipation of catching up with his sisters in Alexandria.

I became more and more exasperated with his repeated refrain. Our Mother Russia is the only way out. Communist Russia will save us from our sectarian fighting, the strife between Christians and Muslims. The greatest mistake that the French made was to decide that the president of this country would be a Maronite. Their worst error . . . . If they had given the presidency to the Orthodox then what you are seeing now would never have happened. The Latin-rite Christians simply do not understand these people of ours. It was their gravest error . . . .

And one day I simply gathered up my belongings, picked up my bag, and stopped in the kitchen doorway with words of goodbye. In his eyes I saw genuine terror. Why? he asked me as he gripped the long handle of the copper coffeepot to move it off the flame. Dressed only in his white underthings, his hair mussed, his appearance invited sympathy.

I'm going to check on the house, I told him.

Fine, he said. But leave your things here. Go on, and then come back at whatever time you wish.

My spirit failed me. I left my suitcase in the entryway, and before closing the door behind me I heard his cheerful voice: I'll make stuffed zucchini and eggplant for dinner tonight.

The service taxi let me out at Starco. I bought some soft white cheese, hard goat cheese, cucumbers, tomatoes, and eggs, and several round loaves of bread, and started up the stairs, thinking about Hanoun and asking myself whether he would revert to his routine of visiting me at home or would leave me to my own devices. I guessed that he would use the suitcase as an excuse. On the pretext of returning it to me and demanding an explanation for my sudden disappearance he would return to his habitual clinginess, fleeing his loneliness and his fear of remaining alone at home.

I did not even notice what had happened to my front door until I tried to fix the key in the lock. When I pushed it in, I found only a hole in the wood of the door. I took a step back. The door had been stripped from its hinges, too, I could see now, and the panel that had been fixed in place now swung freely, lacking a bolt. I pushed it and went in to find the sitting room completely bare. For a moment I thought I had gotten the floor wrong and so I started to retreat quickly to the landing. But just then I became aware that a woman holding a child in her arms stood inside facing me, and at the same time I sensed the hand of our neighbor Abu Adnan grasping my arm and leading me wordlessly to his apartment on the third floor.

Outside the building once again, as I leaned against the wall fronting the Ecole de l'Alliance, Abu Adnan's words paraded through my head, the explanations he had offered, all of which amounted to the fact that my home was no longer mine at the present time; that the people who lived there were not the same ones who had stolen its contents; that I should never have left it so without delegating someone to protect it; and that my only recourse now would be to pay a visit to the youths over at the roadblock on Rue de France next to the church of the Capuchins. They could advise me.

Yet again I found myself taken unawares by the hollowness I felt inside and by my refractory inability to react. As usual, I told myself, I would need time to take it all in.

I remained there for hours: standing in the street, leaning against the wall of l'Alliance. Then I decided that I might as well walk somewhere. On the point of tossing away the sack of food I had bought, I hesitated and then found myself opening it, fishing out a cucumber and biting into it. I started off, swinging the bag back and forth as if I were just a man taking a pleasant stroll along the Corniche on a fine day off from work.

I remembered that I had left money in the apartment. Of course it was long gone now. I could always go back to Hanoun's place, I mused, but the idea did not please me at all. I instructed myself instead to keep walking in this sunny, pleasant weather, toward Wardiye, with a stop at the bank on the way to withdraw some money. At the bank, though, I waited and waited. The employees at this branch did not know me, unlike those who worked at the branch near my home in Bab Idris, which had been closed due to the events. The teller advised me to return the next day, early, so that he could devote his attention to me. He would transfer my Lebanese pound account to a dollar account, he explained. Otherwise—and shockingly soon—my entire worth would not even amount to the price of a decent suit of clothes, he said. I thanked him and put the lire in my pocket. Emerging into the daylight, I began to inspect my clothes, wondering what the man had intended by alluding to "a decent suit of clothes." I figured that what I wore was not in fashion. True, my suit was quite old; but the entire monthly salary of a bank employee would not cover the expense of the material out of which it was cut, not to mention the cost of having it made up. My suit conjured the generation of Théophile Khoury, when you paid only a quarter of a pound for one suit and profited with two!

With the surroundings calm and the weather so fine, I found myself returning to Wadi Abu Jmil. But no, I said to myself, no—what is taking me back to that street? I turned in the direction of Rue de France and began walking through the veritable maze formed by the narrow, tiny lanes. The more deeply I penetrated, the poorer appeared the residents and the sparser were the pedestrians. I knew I was lost when the alleys became completely deserted and all of the buildings were burned out, but surely I was not far from Starco now, and Rue Wadi Abu Jmil must be behind me. Then suddenly I was facing a formidable wall built up with enormous barrels, piled atop one another, wild grasses shooting from their crowns.

Rather than turn back I squeezed myself between the edge of the wall and the lowest layer of barrels and slipped out on the other side. A high dirt mound faced me. When I heard shouting and firing from behind me, I froze in place. A few minutes later I turned, burrowing into the tall grasses and bushes. I circled round the hill of dirt and walked cautiously a little way forward amongst the rocks. I was in a vast empty space. The silence told me that I had entered the city center. I don't know what propelled me on. Perhaps it was the silence, the fact that I could not hear any explosions or the report of big guns, or even the whistle of bullets. I walked for a long time because I did not recognize any landmarks, and in the end I got lost.

That was how, after about an hour of searching, I found myself in front of our shop as the sun dipped toward the horizon.

I live now as I always have wanted to live, surrounded by everything I have wished to have around me since childhood. I see what I want to see and touch what I always dreamed of touching, hearing its rustle, longing to drink in its fragrance, all of the fragrances, filling my eyes with its light and shade.

The day I arrived at our shop—months ago now—I found its contents reduced to little heaps of ashes. I could not see them clearly, for the night had begun to lower curtains of darkness and the walls of the shop, blackened by the fire, made it doubly difficult to see anything of the interior.

I went out again into the street and sat down opposite the shop on a small boulder that I found in the middle of the lane and rolled with my foot to the facing wall. I shook my head in sorrow at losing the income that the shop's old inventory would have yielded, and asked myself what had driven my return to this place. In what condition, after all, had I expected to find the shop?

I felt no urgency about seeing to my own circumstances before the nighttime was truly upon me. We will see, I told myself; after all, I'm fine right now. The weather is spring-like, it's warm, and it would not even be a problem to have to spend the night here. There is not a single person around to fear, not the least sign of weapons—why, there is no one in the entire souq. I opened my sack and took out a loaf of bread. I lay one split half on top of the other, balanced on my arm. On top I lined up some bits of crumbled cheese and rolled it all up, using the plastic bag as a plate. I tore off bite-sized morsels of the sandwich, biting into the tomato between every mouthful of bread and thanking my Lord that I had carried the bag with me all day long and had not tossed it into the garbage after Abu Adnan told me that my home was no longer mine at the present time. I stretched out and leaned my head back against the boulder on which I sat, covering myself with my wool jacket.

It was the chirping of birds the next morning that woke me. Birds! I must be dreaming, I told myself. I have not seen these strange creatures in the city sky for such a long time, ever since the war began, in fact. I got up in a tranquil mood. In the peculiar silence that met me I stared hard at my surroundings. I went into the shop. Next to the black and gray-white ashes, I spotted mounds of variously shaped pebbles, odd-looking in their hues and rounded shapes. It did not take me long to realize that they were lumps of nylon that had burned and melted into little mounds, the remains of the assortment of cheap fabrics that my father, after long and painful thought, had decided to stock. He had cleared all of this ground floor for the cloth. For by that time it was only occasionally that he spoke of true cloth—as he used to call it. Only when the occasional man or woman of some standing appeared, someone who was worth accompanying down to the lower level.

The lower level. The lower level.

I wheeled round to face the back of the shop, which had lost one wall. I uprooted a tiny sapling that had taken root and pushed its way up through the floor. With the aid of a truncated iron rod I began to strike at the mounds of molten synthetics plastered across the metal trapdoor that gave access to the lower level. I went on assaulting them until I had broken the door hinges and could push the trapdoor completely off its wide opening, so that daylight could enter. I stretched full length on the floor and dangled my head down. A cold slap of air hit my face. But it makes no sense, I said to myself as I scrambled to my feet and hurried down the stairs.

Everything was where it should be. It was just as it had been back then when I used to cast a final glance all round every evening before turning out the lights and locking the trapdoor. I had done exactly that on my last day of coming to work in the souq.

Yes, everything was just as it had been. Not even a trace of dust. I did not need to touch any of the tightly-rolled bolts of fabric to be sure of that. From the unique gleam sent off by each textile, each distinct weave, I knew. This was the glow that each one gave off when no dust blocked its pores. It was the particular luminosity of each cloth that I sought and found. I know that light so intimately that for decades the pupils of my eyes have been able to sort out the different fabrics effortlessly.

I think it was the most beautiful moment of my life, yes, since my birth. I clambered up the steps quickly to the ground floor, my heart pounding hard. I came out of the shop, pondering what I had found. Then I began to search the length of Souq Tawile, coming and going, for a living soul. No one. I was sorry now that I had removed the trapdoor completely, and I decided to replace the hinges so that no one could tell. I hurried back to the shop, went inside and then came out again to sit on the rock opposite the yawning doorway that gave onto the street. There was no longer a door at all. I found no trace of the old wooden doors. They must have burnt to nothing, the glass exploding to become fine dust. The sliding metal gate had buckled in the flames and perhaps also because of the bombing that had laid waste to the entire street. The gate had been lifted parallel to the asphalt, and in one corner it was nearly perpendicular to the wall of a building.

I sat on my rock until evening, thinking it all over. The cloth I had found in the cellar, still in fine condition, would guarantee me a livelihood to the end of my days if I were to sell it. It would probably bring enough in to rent a new shop in Mar Ilyas or Ashrafiye and to live my life at a slow enough pace, just as before, settled near the shop. A bedroom, a sitting room, and a kitchen, all for a modest rent.

I was sleepy before nightfall, but the vague fear that had crept into me kept me from descending to the lower-level showroom to sleep. Apparently I was not yet ready to take that step. I replaced the trapdoor over the opening as best I could and returned to my rock just outside. Before I drifted off, I suddenly had the unpleasant thought that rats or mice could have reached the cloth, with disastrous results; they would have ruined it entirely. No, that was improbable, I told myself. I would have sensed it. I would have seen it. So I slept reassured.

I spent many days, perhaps weeks, without daring to leave Souq Tawile. When the battles had stopped after what they came to call the Two-Year War, I had not gone to walk around the city center as so many others had. I had not strolled through the city as so many folk had, dressing their children in Sunday best, making sandwiches and packing cold drinks and roasted seeds, and going off to sightsee in the silent wreckage that so shortly before had been a scene of unceasing tumult and unbearable crowds. I found them appalling. They were letting their ears savor this zone devoid of commotion and car horns, of the noise of motors, the whistles of traffic police, the calls of itinerant peddlers and the yells of those with street stalls. Before, the noise level had been so bad that the vendors had begun to use battery-operated loudspeakers as if they were roving army scouts.

No, I did not promenade with them. Instead, I perpetually postponed my visit to the souq to inspect the shop. And then the war broke out again. As it flared up, I told myself that there had been no incentive to go, anyway. What was the use of inspecting and inventorying the ruins? The only profit I could possibly earn would be an aching heart.

I spent many days, perhaps weeks, standing in front of the chasms that had once been shops in Souq Tawile. It was not an easy matter to recollect their names or owners—even for me, who had grown up there. The walls of those shops now provided fertile ground for grass and weeds. As for the establishments located in wide-open spaces and in direct sunlight, foliage had taken root there, mostly castor-oil plants, and now covered the area. How was it possible? I asked myself. From where had all of this fertility come to the land: where had the asphalt gone? Had the missiles plowed it away? Or had it been the work of wreckage fallen from buildings, which was then dragged across the terrain by rains that washed the rocks bare to raise on this earth a new land? Or, I wonder, had I been suspended from the passage of time, unaware of time's passage, ever since the events had begun and then had been transformed into war?

Raised in these narrow alleys, I no longer knew whether the medlar tree whose fruits had now been nourishing me for weeks had stood near the Antabli fountain for as long as the souq had been a souq, or whether it had grown and borne fruit in my absence . . . in the concerto of this Garden of Eden that the Lord had set aflame to conquer the destruction, to obliterate it and triumph over it. To return sovereignty to the soil.

Let the face of this city be turned under once again, that its inhabitants may leave and new people assume the tending of it.

Crunching pine nuts mixed with ice shavings I take another of my little gulps from the glass of julep, asking myself how Maître Antabli had come upon his blend of sugariness with the fragrance of incense. And whence had he contrived this winy tint to his julep, a luminous red shimmer with a remarkable limpidity that none of the famous julep-masters, not even al-Dimashqi, had attained. No, not even the Damascene master, who had opened a shop in a corner of the Souq des Francs and had dispatched threatening messages to Maître Antabli, all the while boosting the quantities of pine nuts and raisins for customers who showed a readiness to undergo the experiment.

With every swallow I studied the level of the liquid in my glass, enjoying my progress even as I sighed over its dwindling remains . . . until the moment when the words of my father held me in their power. For whenever my father began to talk to me of the grandfather whom I had never known, whenever his eyes filmed over with that delicate veil of longing that drops over people's gaze when they look into the distance and forget who is beside them as they try to remember, I forgot everything too. Then the face of my grandfather would come to me—the face I had invented out of my head, crafting its features to resemble my father's demeanor but adding a measure of severity and a few years.

My grandfather used to say that a city built by Saturn—as the ancients told it—will not flourish long. The opulence of its life blazes only momentarily before it collapses on itself. Hence, on the threshold of the way down to the lower level of the city—threshold to another gate that had vanished, worn down to nothing—the Greeks had inscribed: He who enters this door, let his memory run with compassion. In the days of the Assyrians, the Persians, and the allies of Alexander the Great, the city was brought low. It remained a field of ruins for seventy-five years, until Pompey renovated it, naming it Felicia after his daughter Julia Felix. In her era the great law school was built, to grow to greatness in the age of Alexander Seferos, for it was supported by hundreds of small schools. Its star began to shine brightly and it was named the Nourisher of the Law, but then it was hit by an earthquake and the ground upon which it sat was upended.

In the wake of the wars of the early Muslim rebels and the passing of the troops of Mu'awiya and Yazid, the sons of Abu Sufyan, stability and security reigned until the end of the ninth century. The Emir Nu'man ibn Amir al-Arslani assumed rule, and fortified its walls and castle. Judges, imams, and merchants flooded in, until there came the day upon which it was stricken by another great earthquake. From time to time successive wars shook its foundations without destroying them but also without leaving behind an edifice on which it could flourish and its commerce could grow brisk. It was laid siege by Baldwin, king of the Franks in the age of Sa'd al-Dawla al-Tawashi, who had ripped out its paving-stones, fearing the astronomers' warning that his steed would stumble and he would die. But it was Baldwin himself who died in Beirut, before it was surrounded by Salah al-Din the Ayyubid. And whatever the sieges of Baldwin and the Egyptian navy had left behind was plundered. Salah al-Din had its vines cut down, and its olive trees too. Its monuments were destroyed.

Don't fret, my father would say. And don't stare like that. What your grandfather related to me happened long ago.

My grandfather would say that the Franks had always held fast to their dream of ruling the city. They mounted raids on its populace whenever they could so that no tranquil life could be had. In the era of al-Muqaddam, a Frankish prince—in fact a German prelate also known as 'der Kanzler'—their power merely grew. Al-Malik al-Adil—the 'Just King' of the Muslims—was determined to break that dominance, but the battles simply left the great walls destroyed and the fortress in ruins. Houses were razed and the Franks maintained control until the advent of Sunqur the Brave, leader of the armies of al-Malik al-Ashraf Khalil, son of Qalawun. Those armies laid it waste once again—or rather, they ruined whatever still stood—by hurling incendiary lime upon it.

Why, papa? I would ask.

According to your grandfather, this is the life that a city can expect when it is created under the influence of Zuhal—Saturn, the forbidding star.

My grandfather would say, too, that a civilized existence had returned to the city for a span of less than twenty years before it was struck down by plague and the souls of its people perished—whoever, that is, had not been intent on flight. When the earth was purified, those who had left it returned. Reconstructed yet again, the city returned to a state so prosperous that the son of the Doge of Venice made it his destination. Here he sought his pleasures with a large and raucous entourage of retainers. The people of the city disliked the behavior of the arrogant prince enough to set a trap for him and his followers. A blind shaykh killed him by means of a ruse. When the news reached the Doge of Venice, he prepared his revenge. He fitted a fleet of enormous military ships and sent them to the coast off Beirut. They bombarded it and the Venetian soldiers entered the city, burning it, razing it, killing anyone who had not already fled. Now the city remained in ruins for years.

Next came the wars that liberated the Tanukh chieftains and the emirs of Kesrouane, and then the wars between the Bedouin of Yaman and

Qays. In the days of the Emir Bashir Shihab son of Husayn, Beirut had deteriorated to the point of being a deserted village. But Bashir's brothers, and later his sons and grandsons, rebuilt it and made many improvements—until the plague returned and swept all away. After the governor al-Jazzar—the Butcher—fled to the city, taking refuge from the governor of Egypt, wooden Muscovy ships surrounded it on the orders of Zahir al-Umar; the sailors plundered it and burned its structures. And because the Butcher rebelled against the commands of the Emir Yusuf and betrayed his promise to deliver it to him, the Muscovy ships reappeared off Beirut—again at the request of Zahir al-Umar—and laid siege by land and sea, bombarding it continually, night and day for four months.

And next, my grandfather would say, came the wars between the Muslims and the Christians; and then the city was devastated again by the Egyptian troops of Ibrahim Pasha; and those soldiers could be budged only by the guns on the ships of the European powers, in alliance with the soldiers of that dweller in paradise, the blessed Sultan Abdülmecid Khan. After the Ottoman state transferred the seat of its governorate from Saida to Beirut and put Selim Pasha in charge as Vali, conditions improved. Indeed, life flourished. Consuls and European merchants flocked to it, as did every itinerant and newcomer. The English soldiers remained stationed in the city for a time after chasing the Egyptian troops out of Syria. The rise in rents fueled a building expansion that extended beyond the old city walls very rapidly, to the point where many of those who knew that time well said that Beirut's rapid progress might have been unrivaled by any city in Europe itself. Its population swelled with the folk of the villages, who fled to the city as civil war broke out in the countryside. The continuing brilliance of Beirut's growth was only enriched further by the wars in the mountains between the Druze and the Christians. But in the year 1860, aggressions around Damascus, Wadi al-Taym, and the environs of Beirut itself not only damaged property but began to paralyze commerce as well. Yet the city's numbers swelled, as new inhabitants streamed in and those wanting to rent multiplied. Then the French military arrived and the commissioners moved in to turn the Lebanon into a province independent of Ottoman Syria and directly under the control of the Sublime Porte in Istanbul. Now Beirut witnessed the sort of florescence that is rarely seen. A secure road to Damascus was opened under the aegis of a French construction firm. The city was made a center for Europe's communications with all of Greater Syria, expedited by Ottoman Central Bank accommodations. Beirut went from strength to strength when it officially became an autonomous province, my grandfather explained. Schools sprang up mushroom-like: the Greek Orthodox School, then the Roman Catholic, the Syrian College, the American Protestant College, the Collège des Jesuits, then the Maronites' Hikma School, those of the Lazarist nuns and the Soeurs Prussiennes, Mrs. Thompson's English School, the Nazarene Sisters' School, and the Sultanic Military Institute . . . all of this coming in step with massive urban growth and the founding of presses, newspapers, and magazines.

And that, said my grandfather, relating it from his father, that is when the family decided to leave for Egypt, hauling a wealth of the country's most important export: silk, as well as expertise in its manufacture and weighing, which the people of Beirut had acquired from the time of the Emir Mansur al-Shihabi.

His father did not immigrate to Egypt for the sake of commerce alone, my grandfather would insist, but rather because he was calculating the likely arc of Beirut's florescence. Its ruin was nigh, his father would predict; the age of opulence would run its span and collapse. There was no doubt about it, he would say.

And my grandfather believed it too, just like his father before him.

Why? I asked my father, when Beirut is prosperous and thriving?

Because your grandfather believed that the cycle of life runs to a self-evident rhythm in this city. And because he believed that Beirut's existence would regain its vitality only after passing through colossal destruction and massive death. Beirut's soil is composed of layer upon layer of lives that have passed on. Beirut's soil is not like the soil of other cities, living by the movement of the winds along their surfaces, shifts that shape their edifices but do not pierce deep inside.

Your grandfather's conviction stemmed also from a closely-held jealousy of those who had remained, those who were able to live on in Beirut. His own father's stubbornness, barring him from return, consumed your grandfather. His beliefs arose from his yearning and his love for this city, forbidden to him and so distant. I understood all of this. And here we are, living in this city, secure and well. Don't fear a thing, son.

All that aroused my father's grief in his old age, everything that summoned the aggressive prophecies of his father and grandfather—all of it has disappeared.

All that was on the ground floor has gone to ashes, along with everything that invaded the shop, coming in waves, arriving as if in spite of his will, and instilling a sort of shame and a sad indifference, a renunciation in his last days of all that he had spent his life in loving and knowing so minutely that he followed its every achievement and anecdote. He would gaze at me, seated beside him near the electric heater, and shake his head in regret. When I inquired—What it is, papa?—he would hesitate; and then, playing down the importance of his words, he would say: No, it is the times that have changed. It must be my age. I'm like other old folks, satisfied only with the past and unable to see anything but ruin and inadequacy in the present. Now, conditions are such that you're a cloth-trader, nothing more. In your shop, you sell goods that are made by no one, merchandise that has no history . . . you don't even know what it is made of or where it has come from. You're only a simple retailer who reckons his capital and profits . . . who sells and buys. So it is. You know our old friend Hajj Akbar Maktabi. You recall that when he talks about carpets you can see, as if with your own eyes, his Persian ancestors bent over their folios. You can see them recording their knowledge, the adventures they met in their travels, and the customs of remote peoples—from their manner of knotting the wool ends to their dyeing techniques and on to how they calculate the numbers of stitches according to their religious beliefs. Now compare Uncle Akbar Maktabi to the itinerant carpet vendors who rove around the square at the Burj, carrying a German rug slung over one shoulder as if it is a knot of colored balloons for the children, or a basket of dried figs— it's all the same!

My father would shake his head sorrowfully as he ate chestnuts or drank his tea, not even getting to his feet in welcome should a customer enter the shop. That would throw me off balance. I would hesitate, and then stand up, waiting to hear her requests. Her eyes might roam across the shelves; most likely, she would leave without so much as a word, in which case I would return to my chair next to my father, to sit down silently, putting my hands toward the electric heater.

My father did not live to see the blessed sight of his son sweeping the ashes from the ground floor: nylon, polyester, Diolen, acetate. Unpolished mercerized thread, synthetic wool that blisters under a strong sun, satin that crackles with static in the light, voile that yellows on contact with an odor and creases when hit by a breeze . . . viscose, Rhovyl, Crylar . . . imitations that began with Terylene and sank to a new low with Diolen.

Now, that ground-floor space is my charming verandah. I chop up sharp-tasting shoots of sorrel over leaves of chard and wild chicory. I gaze around, admiring it, finding everything to my liking. The only wild plants I have kept are some ferns. The trellised vines I moved, tiny roots and all, from neighbors' walls, replanting them in the little crevices of my own walls. That is also how I acquired the two miniature sumac trees. I put them on either side of the entrance, next to the basin of wild mint and the laurel with its most appetizing aroma.

After lunch I will walk as far as Avenue Foch after making sure that the entire area is empty; but from Rue Allenby I will turn into Rue

Abdallah Bayhum, not into the avenue where the City Hall sits, as I did last time. There I picked a bowlful of big blackberries, promising myself to return in a few days when a new crop of the delicious berries would have ripened.

This evening, my route will take me by the façade of the Restaurant Ajami. I'll walk down Rue Khan Fakhri Bek as far as the Majidiye Mosque, or south to the Samatiye cemetery. An idea has been circling round my head for some time now, a rather diabolic thought. I so long to see the ocean and to eat fish, and the desire is getting stronger, along with my reliance on God and the fishing hook that I made myself. I prepared it for use several days ago.

Yet when the din of explosions intensifies and fiery blazes fill the sky over the souqs, coming and going over my head and echoing all around me, I prefer to retreat to my house as night falls. These sounds still bother me even if they no longer have the power to frighten me in the slightest.

My house, I call it. My palace, I really should say. I live in a palace such as not even Harun al-Rashid enjoyed, if I am to judge by my reading and what I've always heard. Because, after I undid the ties and unrolled the tight bolts of cloth from their spools, I began to work my imagination. I let my desires guide me as I arranged and furnished my home, spurred on by an irresistible ecstasy. Every time I took down a bolt of fabric—these rare and precious pearls of mine—I spread it out on the floor and began to consider it from a distance, examining it from every angle, wherever the light might touch. I all but wept, my happiness and awe were so great, before coming forward to touch the material. Then I would take off all of my clothes and wrap myself in the length of fabric. I would spend an entire night shrouded in each one. I would breathe in its fragrance and hear its rustle from inside; I would press it against my skin, against every part of my body, to resuscitate my own intimate memories of that particular fabric in every detail—to go back, as if re-reading this memory of mine, finding there the features and elements of this bolt of cloth, page after page . . . word by word . . . letter by letter. At dawn I would awaken inside the cloth, emerging from it to study it again in the new light as it rose, and then in every shift of the sunlight as it hit the cloth and permeated it, until after noontime and on—to the sunset itself. Only then would I refold it or roll it back onto its spool, putting it aside to move on to another one.

So it went, until I came to the end of the cloth, every bolt. I carried all of them up to the ground floor. In the light of day I looked closely at every one and left them all to air for a full day. I began to return the bolts to the lower level one by one, deciding where to place each along the ceiling and walls and floor. I used some of the shelving as framing for a wide bed and chairs, and with more shelves I made a low table for the center of the room. And according to dark and bright hues I funneled the light coming from above to the interior, distributing it by redirecting the reflection of each fabric according to its luminosity or opacity since every fabric either drinks in the light or repels it. According to the degree of coldness or heat inside, I could shift individual bolts of cloth so that my home's temperature would remain moderate, pleasant, and healthful whatever the weather outside, however the humidity thickened or dissipated in the breeze.

Some of the spools—especially the old ones made of bone—I made into water pipes, channeling the water to the interior from the small streams that I sometimes found near the stone bench at the shop entrance. Later, I thought, I would draw water from further away, and perhaps I would even dig a well, as soon as my garden seemed ready.

My mother loved dresses, but not fabric. She delighted in arranging the table, but hated to cook. Mother loved her operatic voice, rather than loving to sing. She did not lie, but it pleased her to compose and recompose life as she wished.

The seamstress to high society, Madame Rahme, came to the house periodically, bringing lengths of cloth that my father had already selected for my mother's special-occasion gowns. From the huge leather case that resembled a doctor's bag Madame Rahme pulled out fashion magazines. She drew her chair close to my mother's, they pushed away the coffee cups, and a long discussion began. Usually, Madame Rahme emerged from this debate exasperated, even furious, but she always held her emotions under her veneer of extreme politeness. She uttered a mounting avalanche of French expressions in the belief that her choice of language would lighten the impact of her words on my mother, who could not find a single outfit in the fashion magazines that pleased her intact. Instead, it would be the collar from this dress with a sleeve from that one, until in the end she had invented something that Madame Rahme might well not be willing to execute, at least not until after considerable negotiations and some downright haggling. At that point they would sit down anew to paper and pen, leaving to me the pleasure of riffling through the magazines, gazing at those women, all so slender that it was hard to imagine them walking in the street without breaking at the waist—thin, smiling women, gesturing as if to explain a difficult but lovely idea to a crowd of listeners. My happiness would be complete only when Madame Rahme rose and went over to the cloth, turning it this way and that, throwing it over my mother's figure or wrapping it firmly around her, then stepping back from her slightly to consider her silhouette from a number of angles as she tossed her gray head to right and left. Only then did she begin to mark and cut with the aid of her small cake of yellow soap, a box of straight pins and the measuring tape which she hung round her neck, as wholly intent on her measuring and her calculations as any skilled engineer or architect. She tossed the scraps of cloth to me and I always gathered them up hurriedly before my mother could pitch them one by one into the rubbish bin, venting her severe annoyance at the chaos that ravaged her life on sewing day, in the front parlor of our home, which was always so neatly arranged and perfectly tidied.

I would take the cloth scraps between my hands, closing my fingers hard around each one, bringing them against my ears. Then I would open my hands quickly to hear the scraps' secret rustling. I would breathe them in, eyes closed, capturing their smell before that wonderful, original fragrance could disappear to be replaced by something akin to the smell of paper or of clothes that have been worn: the aroma of soap or perfume or the human body. There—I crawl behind the couch before my mother can take them from me angrily. I stare at their gleam as I move them little by little away from the source of light. I close my eyes slowly and open them suddenly so that this lovely light will be imprinted on my imagination when I recall it in the night, alone, before I doze off and after my mother has removed from every part of the house the traces of Madame Rahme's passage.

My mother was not fond of fabric. When choosing her clothes, she did not give any thought to the material's weight or density; she did not consider its draping qualities. She paid no heed to how well it would mingle with or lie next to other fabrics. Madame Rahme was visibly offended at my mother's attention to color alone, which she seemed to take as some sort of human injustice, rendering my mother almost incapable of being wife to my father, the man who knew textiles, who understood cloth to such a high degree . . . .

One day, Madame Rahme's disaffection reached such heights that she began to collect her things when my mother requested a collar lined with viscose rather than tulle so that pressing the white piqué would be easier. Madame Rahme gave my mother a long and unswerving stare. She patted her plaited gray chignon, adjusting it with both hands, and began to pick up her belongings as she said to my mother: Madame, I am so sorry. Khawaja Mitri will explain things to you. And when you are persuaded, you know where to find me. Bonsoir, Madame.

All afternoon my heart was low, while my mother's mood soared. But when my father returned in the evening he found her frowning, her lips pressed tightly together. When he asked her the reason for it, she said: You choose the material, Madame Rahme chooses the cut and the style. And me? Every time I suggest a simple modification to her, she scolds me. I thought she was a seamstress!

No, said my father. She is more than a seamstress, much more.

When my mother explained to my father the exact nature of the disagreement, insistent that Madame Rahme had not considered current fashion and did not know what was modern, my father's face took on a grave expression and my mother had to listen.

Listen to me carefully, Athena, my father said to my mother. Do you know that to put certain things together was—and still is—forbidden in the holy books of the Jews? Do you know, for instance, that those scriptures forbade a man to till his field with an ox and a donkey yoked together to his plow? And that it was forbidden to wear cloth woven from two fibers of different origin? This is so not only to avoid bringing together what God has kept apart. More important, it is because to combine, in itself, is a venture of uncertain outcome. The experiment might fail, and leave behind loss and regret. Or it might succeed and yield a harmonious result that is positive, but its very success might produce danger as well, for it might make people arrogant. It might give them notions of being more powerful than they really are, leading them to corrupt the essence of things, of whatever their hands touch.

Ohhh, sighed my mother.

Listen carefully, now, Athena. What most distinguishes Madame Rahme is that she does not march to fashion. Taste and good judgment do not in any sense bow to what you call 'fashion.' Did you know that the word *moda*, the idea of 'fashion,' originated in the courts of the Italian and French princes, where it appeared between the thirteenth and

fourteenth centuries to popularize very expensive cloth and to spread the habit of wearing it, all to the benefit of commerce? That is, 'fashion' was a ploy to sell more widely what had been restricted until then to the sacred garments of bishops and kings, giving it the prestige that accrues to a possession that is accessible only to the mighty and the rich. Only from the middle of the last century did 'fashion' become a matter of repetitive loss of memory, for that was when the repugnant combinations began, the mongrel blends. That is when shops selling 'nouveautés' began to spring up, spreading the heresy of selling cloth next to mass-produced items of identical measurements, and where minor shopkeepers sold anything and everything to anyone and everyone. Before the garment industry emerged, introducing its ready-made sizes—clothes that do not know a body, do not acknowledge each body's distinctiveness—before the clothing manufacturers imposed 'fashion,' and certain types of apparel, on those who made the fabrics, and turned this practice into the natural way of doing things . . . before all of that, we in the East, the skilled artisans of textiles and weaving, were coming ever closer to perfecting our craft. We were making fabrics that were increasing in beauty, while the tailors were refining their expression of the unique relationship between the cloth and the body that yields the ideal form and look.

Oh, come now! exclaimed my mother, who had heard all she could bear to hear. If we were still among the rich, then I would be choosing my clothes ready-made, as the ladies of society do.

We are not among the rich, said my father. So we are obliged to conciliate Madame Rahme. And viscose does not replace tulle in the lining of collars. Not yet. Not yet, Athena.

We were not wealthy during my father's lifetime, but that was not why he continually refused to have a live-in servant at home. Very quickly my mother let go of the idea. Umm Tony from Akkar in the north began to come twice a week, once to clean and once to prepare the more complicated dishes. On these two days my mother would leave the house, claiming that the opened windows and sloshing water harmed her throat. So did the odors of frying and roasting. And after my mother became infirm, to the point that I could not leave her in the house alone all day long and so Shamsa, the Kurdish maid, entered our house, she still grumbled about having the windows opened and complained about the odors of cooking. All day long she pursued Shamsa from room to room, making sure the windows had been shut and watching her closely until she had finished her daily chores. Then she would drag Shamsa to her room, where she was reluctant to let the girl touch anything except on rare occasions and after I had intervened with a measure of firmness. Ensconced in her room, my mother would embark on her stories. Now she told the tales that she had already told so many times, in so many versions that yet preserved a kernel of truth, to Shamsa, who promptly would fall asleep as she sat cross-legged on the floor. In the evening, when I entered my mother's room I would find her singing her operatic voice exercises. I would give Shamsa's shoulder a light shake, causing her to jump—one leap into the sitting room, where she would switch on the television and sit on the floor before it, cross-legged again, while I carried my mother into the bathroom to wash her face with tepid water, removing the powder and the colors that brought on my sadness. I dressed her in her nightgown, fed her, and freshened her face with rose-water before braiding her hair and tying it with a white satin ribbon. I put her in bed and drew the cover over her, wishing her a good night and a healthy sleep. I closed the door to her room and went directly into the kitchen where Shamsa would follow me and help me prepare my own supper, unless Abu Salim al-Tabl was on the evening television program. When that was so, I knew that I would be making my own supper. I ate in the sitting room on a little tray, enjoying fully the little bursts of laughter coming from Shamsa, who had lit up my life, composed as it was of a very few windows, all of them so firmly closed.

Today, after drinking quantities of birds' eggs and eating some very tasty roquette I felt so energetic that I convinced myself to take a serious walk to the further end of the Place des Martyrs, as far as the Café Parisiana and, opposite, the shop of Qaysar Amir, king of fireworks, whose fiery play-things must have transformed the sky into a nightlong festival when the explosions set those rockets and firecrackers on fire. Then I made a turn at Zayn, the fresh juice seller, where I had already found and carried off two metal trays that I now used at home. I passed in front of the Café Laronda, then the theater of Shushu the comedian, and went on to Gaumont Palace, the famous cinema that I had not yet entered, though a few days ago I had been inside of Cinema Byblos, where I had taken some plastic sheets that I put over the plants in my garden to intensify the sunlight and heat on cold and wintry days. I did not go inside the Gaumont, though; likewise, I postponed exploration of the Lazarists' building, making do with picking some hollyhocks that were peeking up at the edges, as if in a hurry to come up before their usual season. I would spread them out on my stone bench to dry. I could make an infusion from them that would be excellent in the event of a cold.

I thought about going on as far as the Bint Jbayl Garage and the shop of Abu Said, 'the licorice man,' as we called the jovial vendor of cold *irq-sus*. But I decided to go back, with a stop at St. George's Cathedral before entering the little souq from the Khan al-Baid steps. I had considered this expedition many times, but had let go of the temptation so that the notion could mature in my head. I had ideas about the precious discoveries and intriguing findings that the area would yield. I had also put it off in expectation that the summer would bring dryness to the vegetation there, so that I would find it easier to pluck tall grasses and weeds out by the roots, opening up some of the narrow lanes that had been completely choked by their growth.

When I crossed the threshold of the Mar Jirjis Cathedral the chill inside startled me, though it was the same coldness that I had found so refreshing as a child, my hand in my father's, while with his other hand he wiped the sweat from his forehead. We used to duck inside the church more to escape the summer heat than with the intent of worship and contemplation. But, once inside, we would sit down on one of the wooden pews, immersed in the silence and the fragrance of incense, studying the saints' images and the beautiful icons. And before going outside again we would light a candle, after my father had slipped a coin into the metallic box nearby, his eyes searching vainly for the archimandrite with the lovely voice.

The cathedral was bare. The interior had been badly burned, as had the Grand Theater not far away. But the church must have been cleaned and emptied of all its contents during the spell of calm, for not even any piles of ashes and pebbles remained. I did not find its emptiness especially frightening. It had more the aspect of a winter sports arena or one of the warehouses down at the harbor, emptied of goods. I went forward to the apse, lighter now because the windows had lost their venerable stained glass. The surface under my feet was soft, and in the corners the ground was moist and fresh. The large concave wall of the choir now looked like a hanging garden in full flower, regularly placed hollows dripping wild chicory, mint, and laurel, as if in flowerpots arranged along a verandah. It surprised me to find no ferns, creeping vines, or bushy castor-oil trees, the sort of vegetation that usually impeded my access to the more appetizing plants that always made my mouth water. I undid my makeshift knapsack, a long rectangle of linen. I had knotted two corners around my waist and encircled my neck with the other two. In it I could carry home whatever I hunted, gathered, or was lucky enough to find. I spread it out on the ground and began to lay chicory and mint on top of the cloth.

I had no idea of how it happened: suddenly, I found myself in a dark cavity below ground. The small opening into which I had tumbled was now more than two meters above my head. I peered in all directions, in search of something, anything, that I could use to support myself so that I could scramble up to the opening. But I was so distraught that I could not see a thing. I began leaping into the air, hoping to catch my hands on the edge of the hole, but to no avail. This was useless, I told myself. First I must calm down in order to see clearly and to think through my predicament. Looking around, I saw a set of stone steps not far away, ascending and descending equally into darkness. Surely, if I could break through the surface where they met the ground above, I would be liberated. I tried but got nowhere. I undid the length of wool that I had wrapped around my neck, as usual; the sweat pouring over my skin was making me shiver with the cold. I sat on the ground, waiting for my eyes to grow accustomed to the darkness. Then I looked all around again, hoping to locate an object that I could set solidly on the ground and that would stay firm beneath my feet while I climbed out. I saw nothing but the stone steps, which I began to descend, though filled with unease. These must be the crypts where they once buried the prelates and the saints whose miracles would one day come to light. I descended further. When the darkness was so thick that I could not see, I stopped. My return would be easy, I thought, but the ascent would not lead me anywhere helpful. I put my hands out to probe the dirt walls, continuing on until my feet no longer met steps but rather were on level ground. Surely I would find something here that I could carry up to use in getting out of the hole, even if it were a grave marker or the bones and skulls of those felicitous holy personages. Suddenly I perceived a faint light reaching me, barely sufficient to tell me that I was on something akin to a stone platform. I peered to both sides and then craned my head, searching for the source of the light. Overhead, I saw a glow emanating from the ceiling of what looked like a little corridor to my right. But I guessed that it must be so far above me that it would not help me to walk in that direction searching for an exit. Perhaps, though, it would lead me to something that I could lug back to the point where I had fallen in, beneath the choir of the Cathedral, by now far away from my present location—or at least so it seemed to me.

I must walk, then, toward the light, whose source, in any case, did not seem to be very distant. But before I could start, with my hand to the wall against which I was leaning, I touched a smooth, rounded surface, a texture very different than the roughness of the dirt-coated stones. Very soon I was able to make out the shape of a large terracotta jar, supported on either side by a pair of stubby pillars or perhaps semi-globular rocks. I stood still, gazing at these shapes in utter bewilderment. I decided to scoop out the surrounding dirt so that I could dislodge these objects and take them back with me. Even though they appeared too heavy for me to carry far, I could always break them apart or drag them or . . . .

My arm struck the surface of the jar, or perhaps its protruding lower half, and it shattered, tiny pieces of it falling between my feet. When I knelt down to see more clearly what I had done, my head jerked back and I all but fainted at the sight that met me. I saw a human form, short in stature, sitting cross-legged. The whole torso was leaning back against the half of the amphora that remained intact and was seemingly fixed in the wall's earthen surface.

It was a girl. I could see her hair. I could see the gown she wore, for it reflected the faint light. I stayed exactly in the same position, not daring to move, as if I feared that the slightest stir of air would transform this wonder into dust and soil. The transparency of her delicate skin gave her the aspect of a skeleton, but with her hair and clothes intact, she had more the appearance of a young woman who had just been laid in her coffin.

I stayed in front of her on my knees, incapable of moving. I felt my eyes burning from the intensity of my stare. I closed my eyelids, reopened them, and breathed slowly and cautiously, so as not to defile the still air. I don't know how it was that this girl reminded me of Shamsa, my beloved Shamsa, whom I had not seen for such a long time and whose subsequent fortunes I did not know. Why this figure reminded me of her I do not know, when there was not the slightest resemblance—neither in the figure, nor the length of her hair, nor . . . maybe it was because she sat cross-legged, as Shamsa had always done, her torso erect, looking directly at my face although her eyes were closed. Perhaps that is why she reminded me of Shamsa.

I stayed on my knees, in front of her, for what must have been a long time, for I sensed the coldness stiffening my hands and feet, and I was suddenly aware, as if it had happened all at once, that my eyesight had weakened. The sensation that I was in a horrifying dilemma overwhelmed me again. I tried to turn my mind to thinking of a way out, quickly, before darkness fell completely over this place. I had no choice before me but to head for the meager light, for I had found nothing that could help me return through the chasm in the floor of Mar Jirjis.

Walking as quickly as I could toward the light, sometimes falling and often stumbling, I realized that some unfamiliar, irregularly placed, stone forms were interrupting my path now and again. But I was too anxious, too afraid of staying underground, to slow down enough to examine them. Quite soon I was able to reach the source of the light, which was covered in lush greenery. With ease I scrambled up to the opening, parted the greenery, and walked out.

The sun had not yet set. I started to walk, brushing the dirt from my body and looking in every direction to ascertain my whereabouts. I was not in an open square or an empty stretch that would afford me the breadth of view that I needed to figure out where I was. I seemed to be in a labyrinth of small, crisscrossing alleys. I walked forward with great difficulty, picking my way amongst the many little tree trunks, my progress also obstructed by piles of stones. As small as some of them were, they had accumulated to create a semblance of natural barriers, for the rainwater had washed them into linear mounds. Perched atop one of them I picked some sweet wild tomatoes and wolfed them down. I resumed my meandering way until I recognized my surroundings as Souq al-Nuriye, once I was certain that I was in what looked like the small square in front of al-Nuriye Church. I took a deep breath, suddenly unperturbed. I forgot the business about the girl in the amphora. Here I was, I told myself, at the edge of the little souq, which I had been promising myself to visit, tantalizing myself with its potential. I would return soon, then. I went on walking as far as Souq Sursock, turning in the direction of the Mosque of Mansur Assaf. Now, I told myself, if my memory serves me correctly I need to walk down Rue Husayn al-Ahdab, which leads to the Place d'Etoile, which I can cross to get to the Omary Mosque, then on to Rue Weygand, and home . . . .

But I got lost.

Lost, and I was dead tired. Instead of the square in which the mosque was located, I found myself once again nearing the stairs at Khan al-Bayd and the Abu Nasr Souq. I sat down on the edge of a crumbled wall to catch my breath. I told myself that tension and fear were preventing me from thinking clearly. What was I so frightened of, here? I asked myself. What could possibly summon fear . . . what could cause me this anxiety now? Fishmonger's Square must be behind me, then the Goldsmiths' Souq, and from there I could exit toward Patisserie Hallab or Azar Coffee Roastery, and then go down to Place des Martyrs toward the Rivoli. In moments I would be at home. What are you frightened of,

I asked myself, when night is still slow to fall?

I wonder if it was my intuition. I wonder if I was afraid even before I knew the source of my fear. Had I somehow heard the reason for my fear before my ears actually picked it up?

The sound I heard, as if it had emerged suddenly out of total emptiness, could not possibly be the howling of dogs. It couldn't be. I had never met a dog in this place throughout my entire life here.

The howling rose, sharp and aggressive. It poured into my head, filling it instantly with terror. It is not the howling of dogs, I was saying to myself over and over as I searched frantically for a hiding place, the hair on my head standing on end like the prickles of a porcupine, stinging my scalp.

It is not the howling of dogs. I spit onto my hands to check the direction of the wind, so that I could place myself where my scent would not blow toward them. It was not easy, for every path here led to a dead end, as in a maze. And it would do me no good to rub my body with greenery as a camouflage. I must get up to a high rooftop or into a tree, or shield myself in a hollow or hole with an opening that I could block up, closing myself in.

I found myself leaping, as buoyant as the wind, up the rocks, hanging from iron bars and gashed-open window ledges, rising far above the ground . . . on a level with the crown of a small date palm. I jumped onto the flooring of what remained of a small balcony overlooking a space where several narrow lanes met, and which I imagined to be the little square at the souq where the fishmongers sold their catch. Poking my head out through the ferns, I saw the pack.

I could not make out the number of dogs as they ran, appearing and then disappearing again amongst the alleyways. But soon the pack gathered in the small square, in a bloody fight that ended with two of them wrestled to the ground and motionless. After the howling turned into something more akin to the lowing of bulls, I saw the biggest of them dragging an indistinct mass with his jaws. He began to tear it apart, and then the others caught up to him, and there were no more than ten, as far as I could see from where I stood.

They're wolves, I said to myself, figuring that they were ripping apart the corpse of one of their own, fallen in battle. But the head that rolled away, and toward me, was not a canine head. It had belonged to a human being.

A human head . . . it's a human head. I murmured it over and over in a barely audible voice. O God. Where did they get a human corpse?

Heavy rain was coming down by the time I shimmied inside on my belly and lay there. I don't know how much time went by as I lay there inert. It seemed that I would be spending the night right here; and tomorrow I would certainly be dead. Dogs or people, whichever it might be. Or I could stay imprisoned up here and die of hunger.

Thoughts went through my mind all night long. I did not sleep at all. I was completely soaked, to the bone, and my head was on fire. I considered getting up just before dawn and walking as silently as I could to the nearest bank of sandbags that edged the city center, and screaming as loud as I could to the people who would be crouched behind it. Take me away from here! That is what I would yell as I walked in their direction. They would either open a way for me to escape or they would spray me with bullets as soon as they saw the slightest movement, perhaps even before hearing my voice. I had heard it said that they booby-trapped dogs and let them go at the limits of the city center, so that a sniper from the opposite side would fire at the animals and they would explode in enemy territory. But these were old techniques that they surely had abandoned by now, for I heard no sound of explosions in the vicinity. But I would not be able to follow my plan tomorrow, for at present they were all occupied with the battles whose fierce and strident echoes I had been hearing for several days now.

It was all nonsense, anyway. All nonsense. I would not dare to do anything. I would stay right here, on my backside, until my death. Never to return to my tranquil life, to my little paradise. My garden will die, I thought, and I will not get to say my goodbyes to my fabrics or my home.

At the first glimmer of dawn I returned to the balcony, forcing myself to take a surreptitious peak outside. An infinite calm seemed to have settled on everything around me. I could hear the birds chirping. And in spite of the murky sky, I could see clearly that the square and the alleys beneath me were empty of dogs and of the traces of their battles the night before. I saw neither the bodies of the two dogs nor the human head.

I questioned myself sternly. Had yesterday's scenes come from my disturbed dreams or been the result of the fevers flaming inside my head? I must be ill, I told myself. And in my delirium I imagined things that had no foundation in fact. But I could not get around one question: why had I scaled this bombed-out building? I guessed that the fever had struck before sunset, seized control of my mind and body, and carried me in my senseless raving to this spot.

I had the taste of rusty metal in my throat as I slipped from my lofty hiding place to the ground. I recalled the wild tomatoes that I had eaten yesterday; perhaps they were poisonous. But where would the poison have come from, when they had drunk only rainwater?

I started to walk without really planning my route. I encountered no trouble reaching the street of the Omary Mosque. I paused there to rest my aching joints, assuring myself that I was sick. That was all. My feebleness was only the result of the fever, which no doubt would start again to mount. I began to shiver with the cold as I had earlier. I must eat, I told myself. Right there I commenced to collect some snails. Later I could rinse them in seawater. I would eat them and drink my hollyhock preparation. I remembered my bundle and all I had left inside of it in the Cathedral of Mar Jirjis. And I recalled the young woman in the jar.

As I passed the corner of the Awza'i Mosque I quickened my pace, making my way in earnest so that I would reach home before the rain could get any heavier. And I began to think about linen. I was thinking ardently about the linen that awaited me at home, in which I would wrap myself—in that linen, exclusively. I would wind myself up in that linen and it would cure me. I would warm myself in that linen and I would recover. And I would remember the linen of Shamsa.

Did I fall in love with Shamsa for her linen? At the time when she forsook the cotton of her youth, of her warm, familiar, and gentle childhood, for linen . . . when she put on linen, and to it added a trespasser, the enticement of velvet. Preludes.

One evening she said to me: Tomorrow, I will go to my mother's to spend the Kurdish New Year, the feastday of Nayruz, with my family. I'll come back the day after.

I was taken aback, she saw, by the announcement that she would stay overnight with her family on a day other than Sunday. She knew, moreover, that I would be forced to leave the shop, for my mother could not stay alone. But she merely laughed lightly. I am fully grown now, she said to me. My family will not let me stay overnight here. I must return to them every evening.

I understood then that Shamsa had entered the lunar cycle, that she had joined the caravan of women. How could I not have remarked her body blooming under the loose cotton that she wore? How could I not have detected her new scents? All I saw was that she was filling out and that her body seemed to spill over its limits, growing more generous, rounder. Sometimes, when she rose from the floor suddenly and padded off quickly in her bare feet, I did notice her buttocks quivering beneath the sway of her long, fat braids. I noticed, and smiled, and then I forgot about it.

Tomorrow, my mother will give me my *jayis*—my trousseau.

You are getting married, Shamsa?

She laughed. No. Not right now. But from now on I will wear pretty things, clothes of a different sort. The prettiest ones my mother will hide in the *jayis* trunk until my wedding. Tomorrow, if my mother allows it, I will visit you, to show you and your mother some things.

At noon the next day I opened the door to Shamsa. I was completely taken aback when I saw her. Even my mother began to stammer, the broth dribbling from her chin. Our apartment, always so dark and airless, blazed with Shamsa's colors as if the ceiling had raised its hat and flung it away.

A *shams*, a sun—that is what you are, Shamsa!

Yes, she agreed, laughing. My real name is Hatawi. That is what my family calls me, and it means 'sun,' as *shams* does in Arabic. And this is my grandmother's gown, which my mother has carried with her since she was little.

Shamsa went about showing us her many robes and accouterments. This is my dark-red shawl, and here is the red linen *tjikit*, lined in wool felt. Here is my yellow *bashtamal*, embroidered in flowers. I tie it like an apron under this thick belt, my *futeyh*. It protects my kidneys and spine when I carry heavy loads. Now, this is my *tiri*, this brilliant green robe, split in front and on each side so that I can walk with long strides in the steppe. And under the sky-blue *yalik* that keeps my ribs warm, see, here is my white linen *ishligh*, falling over lilac knickers, *shilwar*, and my stockings, or *ghurik*, also lilac. On my feet, did you notice the leather *teshrek* that we make ourselves, from animal hides?

Look, here is what I put on my head, a red fez or tarbush, and this is my silvery veil, a *bashlak*, decorated with gold coins. Over all of this I throw square scarves, called *bushi*, each one a different color. I knot them all around my temples, leaving one to throw back like a headscarf. But it must never cover my face or my braids.

Princess Hatawi left our home with her wardrobe, leaving nothing behind for me. All of these fabrics that she had put on again, had arranged and bundled up and tied before departing . . . all of these colors over which she threw her dark-red shawl and her white scarf . . . all of this linen, and a little velvet. And she had gone. Nothing stayed behind for me. I had been so astonished, and so full of joy, that I had touched nothing. All day long, my hands held themselves open and my eyes were full of tears. All night long, I tossed and turned in bed, unable to sleep, awaiting Shamsa's reappearance the next morning and swearing deep inside myself that I would find pretexts to prevent her from leaving the house . . . so that I could hover around her, could sniff the aroma of the cloth she wore, here in my own air, could try to touch it. Could try to touch her. All night long, I tossed in bed, a lump in my throat. I do not want to accept the will of her family, their demand that she return every night . . . I will find something, I will find a reason, to prevent her from spending the night elsewhere. How can I bear it, how can I bear nights emptied of Shamsa? And the mornings as well . . . How could I have been so heedless of the grace of her presence in the house throughout the evening and all night long, and in the morning, too? How could I not have felt the blessing of her breathing as she slept nearby, exhaling the fragrance of freshly kneaded dough, as I slept on, ignorant, ungrateful, reprobate? That night, I did not sleep.

My mother awoke. Still in bed, she found me already fully dressed. I had been ready since dawn. Slowly and carefully, I washed her face and cleaned her dentures. I combed and plaited her hair. I brought her sweet biscuits and milk. I carried her into the sitting room and aired out her bedroom. I washed the dishes and dusted. I soaped the washbasin and sprayed cologne on my face. I drank my coffee and washed the cups. I carried my mother back to her bed and put a record she loved on the gramophone. I wrapped my left ankle in a long ribbon of gauze and sat down on the sofa. I stared into space and waited.

And then Shamsa came into the room. As I rose to greet her with a smile, a sort of dizziness struck me. My foot is hurting, I told her. I am not going to the shop. And since I had some time on my hands, I've spared you the housework and I've given mother breakfast. How are you, Shamsa? What are you wearing today? Did you color those blond braids of yours with henna? What do you have on?

All of that linen is for me? For me. All of these layers, those I can see and those I know are there through my imagination, gauze and raw linen for the wounds to my heart. The linen of handkerchiefs that flutter with goodbyes and wipe away lovers' tears. The coverlets from your cradle and the sheets of your trousseau. Give me some of your linen, let me touch it. Lie yourself down inside of it and press it against your body, everywhere. Don't shrink from me like that. Let me stay next to you, here on the sofa, so that I can tell you of linen, recounting things about linen as no one else will. So that I can tell you linen, and tell you the wound in my lover's heart. Will you dress it in gauzy linen?

Listen:

The first to wear linen knew its prodigious curative qualities, for they noticed, Shamsa, that it assists in sealing wounds. They used it to heal leprous ulcerations. Linen became the symbol of purity, and the whiteness of linen grew ever more pure. And even if it did not cure all skin sores, it was the fabric that came closest, the most able to consort with the heat of the skin. Linen is tender, Shamsa. Touch it, and touch my hand, and the tenderness you sense will come alike from both of us. Haven't humans made their bed sheets from linen? Haven't they chosen it to cover their tense bodies, to calm them in sleep, as if they were in the arms of faraway mothers? Slip down a little, toward me. Come nearer, give me the hems of your robes to hold, and listen.

Linen is the child of the four elements, and of the four points of the universe. From the Baltic to the Mediterranean, it is the most ancient and most noble of cloth. From the earth its seeds take their strength. It sprouts in March and in July the plant is gathered. Flax blossoms, quick to disappear, are blue, but only a few hours after they open, the flowers turn the fields golden. Five weeks after the flax buds flower, the plant is cut down from the stalk, like wheat. From its seeds comes fodder for animals, oils, and fats. Does not every part of it yield bounty and goodness?

After earth comes water: for the stalks are soaked until they relax into a tangle of fibers. After seven weeks they have given the water the hue of the setting sun. Then they are left to dry and pop under the flame of the summer sun, to separate the textile fiber from the woody stem. After the fiber dries to a color that ranges from rusty red-brown to grayish blue, it is beaten and threshed to bring the filament out of the fiber.

Those who have suffered, Shamsa, must torment others; but do not torment me. Be as pliant and soft as the filament made delicate . . . a thread so delicate that the light of the sun quickly sullies its whiteness. So that it would remain pure, so that it would not yellow, the flax was spun in moist caverns, its pallor transferred to the fingers of the delicate girls who worked it in the shadows, in a perpetual darkness. But the pale white of the spinner was equaled only by the white shoulders of the Spanish Empress Eugenie, who was first to replace her lacy chantilly shawl of white linen with a black linen mantilla. The shrewd Eugenie preferred that the whiteness of her shoulders not be compared to the whiteness of linen worked in the moist caves, soaked in all the potash of Russia and Poland and then in the pure, clear waters of Haarlem in Holland. To ensure that the linen would not be the victor she had it dyed black, so that against it the luminous whiteness of her shoulders would become legendary . . . . Only the envious Queen Marie de Medici would not acquiesce. To the very last day of her life, it was said, she wore nightgowns of white linen so that the king could never forget that her skin was yet more intensely white. To sleep in white linen became the most extravagant of luxuries, a notion unheard of in the memory of flax.

Linen is noble yet modest, Shamsa, so very much like you. Leave your *ishligh* draped over your body; do not take it off. I want only to look at you, and to talk. Do you know that the Kurds were the first in this region to weave these plant fibers? Yes, your people. The ancient Pliny used to say that to weave linen was honorable even for men, because it took first place over the wool of the pastoralists. Of the earth's nomads only the Berbers remained, and the agriculturalists established towns. Linen became the shroud of the dead laid out in the tomb, when before, corpses had been wrapped in animal hides and buried in fetal position. It was so, even if you continued to be herders and were barred from entering your towns.

In the beginning your linen came from the land of the Persians, as my father narrated the story to me. It entered Egypt and from there Pythagoras carried it to the Greeks. Confucius the Wise, who so loved to read the poems of his favorite book, the *Shijing*, chanted in equal manner the praises of *rami,* the long-fibered hemp of Siam.

Do not be ashamed of your nakedness, visible beneath the linen, for it covers and shields you. Do not hear my desire in my words; hear only my story. Let your skin listen to the linen I tell, so that afterward your silent mouth and your frightened eyes will come to meet me.

Five thousand years ago the Pharaohs, whom Isis taught to weave linen, presented their gifts to her in the form of tiny statues representing the Goddess Hathor—and her hair was made of the fibers of hemp. Of linen, they sewed the sails of their Nile-going boats: the sails of life. And linen's weavers in Egypt were the Copts—according to what my father's father related. Their intercessor was St. Mark, who evangelized Egypt's folk. The Copts feared the brilliant rise of the city of Alexandria, dreading enslavement in its imperial factories. And because they did not follow the Byzantine Church, because they refused to bow to it, they lived on the forgotten margins of Egypt. In weaving, spinning, twisting, and polishing fibers, they found their independence and practiced a pacific resistance that they buttressed by mounting to the rocky heights of Upper

Egypt like their patrons, Saints Antony and Bakhum. Because they were so dedicated and skilled, they turned out linen that was superbly fine, the threads soft and supple. Sometimes they introduced wool at the edges, to give it weight and body, while at the same time enhancing it with embroidery.

Did not Ezekiel say: For you will be the fine linen of Egypt, from which are worked coverlets and tunics. The Arabs reached the Copts' workshops in Damietta and as far as the Delta reached, and from there they exported the tightly-woven linen of the Copts called *pokalemon*, dyed with very beautiful colors that changed according to the temperature and hour of the day. Their glorious textiles were offered to the Fatimid caliphs. From their delicate linen the Copts of Egypt were obliged to make what was later called the *chemise*, worn by the Frankish soldiers under their armor when the sun of the Egyptian Delta had broiled them. Have not the experts counted one hundred and eight threads—doubled—to the centimeter in the delicate Egyptian linen of the pharaonic period? And did not the Copts imitate from these forebears the practice of coating the threads with flour made from certain grains to stiffen it and to bring out the texture of its lacy weave?

Like you, Shamsa, linen was noble, and stingy and lavish at the same time. Like your body, bestowed without effort, recalcitrant in its splendor.

At the end of the fourteenth century, did not the King of France obtain the release from captivity of a European ally held by the Sultan of Turkey by giving the Sultan as ransom a length of the famous linen of the city of Rheims? Did not that same king say that he had no fear for the folk of Flanders as long as they had their fields of fibers, and fingers to spin it, and arms to weave it, and as long as the thumbs were not severed from the hands of the women who wove it? Until the end of the last century linen remained the temptation of queens and the bread of spinners, until the coming of cotton, borne on the revolutions of the century's end. And cotton would bring lower prices, borne on the commerce in herds of black slaves. International trade, especially with America, increased cotton's potency, through pesticides and fertilizers that ruined the earth.

Lacemaking and netting, tulle and guipur, and lace made of linen thread drove the dreams of the Spanish Eugenie until the dawn of this century. But our century's machinery was harsh and rapid, and it broke the heart of linen, too fragile to tolerate its rhythms.

Your linen *chemise* is most precious, Shamsa, and it lies perfectly across your shoulders. But do you realize that its worked surface has come to you from deep inside Egypt's ancient tombs? The first hieroglyph was one thread upon another. The first tablet written concerned the sleeves of garments. The task of mixing air into linen—how to perfectly blend air and thread—would come to fruition only in the city of Venice. At that point it would become lace. This I will tell you another time, when the moment comes for it, and for you.

Shamsa, has the story of linen pleased you? Now you really know what you are wearing. Your body knows it, and moves forward inside it . . . progresses in a knowledge that we have begun to find together, and that we will go on finding together as long as you wish it so. This will be our secret, the two of us, and we will go on with it as long as you desire it.

Valuable and beautiful is your linen tunic, Shamsa, and it lies upon you perfectly. Why do you not undo the knot, loosen the neckline, and push the satin ties away from your ivory neck? Who hennaed your long hair until its blondness turned into such flame?

No—do not give me the fill of your breasts all at once.

Is this whole expanse for me? . . . All of this city, its heart fortified, is it mine?

I . . . I am its only sovereign. I preside over all that is above earth and what lies beneath the surface. My walls are impregnable, more so than any earlier sovereign here has been able to say. As my desires know no bounds, I build and demolish, erect and raze, and whenever I choose, I return to my palace to select my mistress from among the fabrics that await me there. Will she be tender and gracious . . . lascivious and wicked . . . dreamy and idle . . . ignorant and enchanting . . . sweet and just . . . distracted and forgetful of me . . . .

The whole universe is mine, father, I would say out loud, raising my voice in song, leaving it to my legs to run in any direction they wanted.

With my bundle and thick stick, after all, I knew that I had become like the prophets, walking wherever I pleased and desired, for my own distraction and discovery and for the wisdom of the days and nights that I extracted without fear, now that I had assured my sovereignty over this place . . . for a great while.

I stayed for days in a cocoon of linen, drinking my hollyhock and sage. I recovered from the fever that had taken hold of me, and one morning I decided to return to the alleys of the small souq that ran parallel to Place des Martyrs. I would not lose my way this time, I told myself. I would mark my path, and would give new names to streets and markets that I did not recognize. In my head I would draw a new map of these sites that had changed so much, losing their original features.

I entered from the goldsmiths' souq. Earlier, I had carried off some large rocks from this place, out of which I had fashioned a low wall for my garden to protect it from the rivulets of rainwater that had swept away parts of it over the winter. It did not take me long to recognize the remains of Dabbous Herbalists. There I found a true treasure. This time, I was determined, I would not leave it to my return trip to collect things, since perhaps I would choose a different route. Laughing out loud and clapping, I undid my homemade knapsack and spread it out on the ground.

Some seeds—flowering plants and grains—had pierced their tiny outer skins and sprouted in the pumice stone, forming a lovely little windowsill garden. I began to uproot them and arrange them in my bundle, promising myself to make my garden and verandah a true paradise in this lovely summertime. Lifting away some of the rubble, I found a glass jar of olive oil, which I opened immediately. I drank from it, smacking my lips and savoring the little puddles of oil, swishing them on my tongue. Now, I told myself, everything was complete and ready for illuminating my evenings, though I thought it unlikely that I would ever find a match to light the wick. But I forgot my sorrow quickly when, at the shop's broad entrance, I found small shoots of maize that had pushed their way up inside the remains of pipes. They must have sprouted during the season just past. There were a great many of the little shoots, I saw as I pulled them up, and it occurred to me right away that they would probably be enough to form a veritable screen in front of my home and verandah, and to mark out the edges of a passageway between my home and the sea, if I took the path's route in an arc, by way of the Majidiye Mosque.

I promised myself to return to Dabbous.

I hoisted my bundle onto my back and took up my stick, beating hard at the tall, yellowed grass to leave unmistakable markings as I passed. I reached the square where I had sought shelter from the dogs—or fever had made me imagine as much—and I named it Square of the Dogs. I came to the tailors' souq, which I recognized once I had reached the Catholic church, and I estimated that now I was facing Place d'Etoile. Raising my head, I could see the upper rim of the clock face from the tower in the square, facing the Parliament building; the clock's disappearance had left a rusty gap at the crown of the stone pillar. I went out to Rue Maarad, thinking I would go as far as Rue Weygand and from there would go home to plant the shoots before they could wilt. But I changed my mind and headed in the direction of the Mosque of the Emir Mundhir. From there, I told myself, I can reach the corner of the Awza'i Mosque. That way, I will have tried a new route, possibly making some discoveries and useful finds.

Behind the Parliament building, before the intersection at Rue Riad al-Solh, a luxuriant growth of reeds came in sight. I went over to it and found a lake of pure water fed by a little spring. I drank my fill, lowered my bundle from my back, and sprinkled it with water to keep the roots of the shoots and seedlings fresh and vigorous. At the pond edge I scrubbed my hands and face with 'glass grass,' as my aunt called it. She used to stuff this plant into a glass pitcher and shake it until it shone, ignoring my mother's dismissive and scornful comments. It occurred to me that I might as well bathe thoroughly in the pond, before my body cooled down too much as I sat resting. But before I could start, I caught sight of a long white bone. I went over to it and turned it over with my foot, feeling uneasy. It did not take me long to convince myself that it was a human thighbone.

No doubt of it, I was repeating to myself as I knotted my bundle around my waist. No doubt at all, I said, as I walked faster and then ran, returning in the direction of Souq Sursock. But as soon as I reached it, I regretted my about-face hugely. I began swearing at myself and the whole damned day, because I had not thought to run toward the Awza'i Mosque and then home. What had made me flee in the opposite direction of the small area that I knew well and in which I was certain of my safety? Was it my fear of my own ignorance about this particular stage of the route home, of the unknown space between my present location and my home?

I did not retrace my steps toward Square of the Dogs and the human bone, that stark indication that what I had seen on that evening was not the hallucinatory product of fever.

Then I heard a howl in the distance. I ran to the opening in the ground where I had come out after falling into the vault at Mar Jirjis. Supporting myself on my stick, I jumped.

I will not leave my bundle behind this time, I told myself as I rested to regain my breath, certain that the dogs would not be able to follow me here. All I would have to do now would be to return along the underground corridor, taking the stone steps, to reach the amphora girl. And from there I could feel my way to the crypt of Mar Jirjis. I would come out there, this time using my stick to help me ascend, and emerging from the cathedral I would be in the open space that I knew well. I had never yet seen dogs there. I would walk down in front of Azar Coffee Roastery and across Place des Martyrs to the Rivoli and then Avenue Foch, and then straight toward the sea to reach home.

I started to wonder how the barking could have escaped me all of this time. How could I not have heard it? How could they not have sniffed my scent as I meandered through the city center? I wondered whether subconsciously I had assumed that the barking was coming from outside of the city center, beyond the sandbag barrier. Did they prowl only a certain distance, I wondered, through a particular area that they would not leave? Where had they found that person? Was it the one they had torn apart on that ill-fated night, or was it someone else? Had they stalked and then killed the person on the spot, or had they found the corpse elsewhere and dragged it there?

O God, O my God, I said out loud, listening as my voice echoed in the cold, dry underground air. O God, O Mar Jirjis, St. George, Mama, I repeated, walking very fast, poking at the walls and the ground with my stick.

I walked on; it seemed further than I had estimated as the distance to the girl in the amphora. What I was now touching, it seemed to me, was not the side of that same corridor. Suddenly, I collided into an earthen wall. I started to grope about for a breach and then retraced my steps. I found an opening the size of my body or perhaps slightly wider. I hesitated about slipping into it, my body tensed to fit. I decided to proceed very slowly, so that I would not fall into any large apertures that I would be unable to climb out of. The narrow passage sloped downward. Nothing to worry about, I told myself, I'm in control of the situation. I can always shimmy up in the opposite direction, whenever I want. A few minutes later I found myself in something like a small hall. It was not pitch-dark there; or perhaps I had simply become accustomed to seeing in the dark, like a mole. No, it could not be that, not really. I could tell from the density of the air and the echoes of the sounds I was making. In any case, the human brain does not acclimate well to pitch blackness and will not give in to it for any length of time; to compensate, it will invent its own images, and that is what it will see.

So it was that I saw . . . a chamber walled round with what looked like white marble and furnished with sarcophagi, large and small. I probed the wall, keeping close to it as I walked, leaning against it. It led me to a similar room but on a lower level. The sounds I was producing, or my impressions, gave me to see that here there were not sarcophagi but rather upright stones, perhaps statues or small obelisks planted in the hard earth.

I walked on, led by the magic of the darkness, and by what I saw without truly seeing, what I saw by the light made by the illusions of my brain, or by the glow of the white stone walls, or perhaps by a real light coming from the other world above, reaching me by an avenue I did not know. I went on, bewitched by my memory of my paternal grandfather's words. A city that does not advance in time but rather in accumulating layers, a city that will sink as deeply in the earth as its edifices tower high.

How many cities lie beneath the city, papa . . . grandfather . . . how many cities lie there to be forgotten?

I wonder: am I descending through the layers of this city, or am I plunging down, down to submerge myself in the deepest layers of my own illusory thoughts? Grandfather, from whom I inherited the absurdity of wisdom, did you grow so passionately attached to cloth because it will not be here when the archaeologists excavate the traces of our disappearance? Was it because cloth is neither ceramic nor bone, metal nor stone, but just a bit of carbon and dust, like the traces of dust that the muscles of our hearts will leave behind? Because its weave will disappear as quickly and easily as the life of cities like this one, though unlike them its patterns will not leave impresses in the earth's sediments, in the deposit of each successive layer, when the hurried diggers search for the residues of our passing. But it is all the same, grandfather, for God has blessed us with shortsightedness. And sometimes with opaque darkness.

It surprised me that I did not feel especially afraid. I felt no dread about going on and going deeper. I undid my bundle from my back, now chilled by the dampness of the cloth I had sprinkled with water at the pond, and hoisted it over my shoulder. I remembered the dogs, but I forgot that I was fleeing from them. I did not care.

I sat down to rest from the fatigue of making my difficult way forward in the thick darkness. When I closed my eyes, a heavy torpor filled me, rising to my head. I stretched out, put my arm beneath my head, and surrendered to a deep sleep.

When I awoke, my stomach was groaning with hunger. I took a gulp of olive oil and carefully replaced the cork, vowing my determination not to lose today's plunder whatever the circumstances. I reinserted one end of the cloth that wrapped my finds through the handle of the gallon jug, which made it easier to carry. I tied the bundle firmly around my waist and stood up. I must get out now, I told myself, if I am to get home before nightfall, since I have no idea how long my napping here lasted.

I began walking cautiously, my arms outstretched to touch the wall. I walked a curved path a few steps and sensed a decline under my feet. No, I said, I'm still going deeper. I have to change direction and find the point where I can start ascending toward a way out. I turned to walk in the opposite direction but the wall seemed blocked. This makes no sense, I told myself. I have to find the opening through which I came in. I asked myself if my long nap had caused my forgetfulness and disorientation. I stopped going round stupidly in place, to think, to use logic. That is when I heard voices in the distance. Human voices. Were they really human voices?

In any case, I had no choice but to walk on, going as if in spite of myself toward the source of the commotion. I was drawn by the entice-ment of human voices, still apparently far off, and yet I was very afraid of them. I would walk toward them, I said to myself, to find a way out, but I would not actually come out right away. I would stay underground but almost at ground level, and decide then and there what to do.

Walking toward the source of the voices was quite easy to do. Or per-haps it was just that I was trying so hard to marshal my tense nerves so as to focus my ears on the voices that it merely seemed so simple. I knew that I must be close, for the air had grown warmer and less stagnant. My eyes soon made out a faint light reflected at the feet of the low walls far in front of me. I began to walk quickly, my mouth open so that the sound of quick breaths into my nostrils would not bury the sounds that my ears were picking up.

I stopped so that I could better hear. Still as a stone, I could hear clear-ly the crash of waves breaking. Could I have reached a spot near the shore? Of course not, I told myself; it is just the sound of big waves, carried by the wind. That did not so much mean that I was near the shore as it told me that the ocean was rough today and the wind was strong, even though it was still summertime.

Then I heard a powerful rumbling and the earth above me shook, dirt raining down over my head. I froze, and stayed right where I was, as rigid and immobile as a rock. This was a rumbling that I had not heard before . . . a strange rumbling that I had not heard. Had I walked—underground—beyond the sandbag frontiers, I wondered? Had I entered war territory without knowing it?

The light and the noise were coming from somewhere not far above me. The vibrations in the earth above followed the line of the rumbling. It was a tank or an armored car, then. That meant I was outside of my own territory. And I must turn and go back immediately. Immediately . . . and before the humans above discovered that hole in the earth so near to my position, and discovered the ground that lies underground.

As rigid and immobile as a rock. Under the hole, not far away, lies a bulky missile. Sleeping on its side like the corpse of a dolphin. Whole, sleek, swollen. A layer of dirt covers it. Dirt above, and the rumbling on the surface.

How much time went by? The sun had not yet set. The rumbling stopped, having grown more distant. No debris would fall on the missile and so it would not explode.

Then I heard the voices. Shouting, clamor. Human voices and the staccato clatter of machines. Metallic human voices. Splintered and shattered, vibrating, muddled. Words that I could not make out.

Laazazel. Lehesha Er. Lehesha Er. Kess ekhta.

Could this be my fever returning, I wondered? Did a feverish delirium capture my head whenever terror infiltrated my body?

Zeherot. Zeherot. Lolazoz. Lolazoz. Mokshim. Ben Zena Lehesha Er.

What was I hearing? What language was that? Who was talking, above me? Which devils were these? What distance had I walked, underground, that I now found myself in another country? What people had filled the land beyond the center city limits, and now drove their rumbling armored cars across it?

Rigid as a rock, until they were distant and their voices had faded, along with the rumbling and the metal jangling.

I would not come to the surface here. I would not let the light tempt me, nor the total silence that had now returned and permitted the rhythmic sound of breaking waves to come to my ears.

I shut my eyes tightly. I kept them closed for several moments so that I could more easily walk quickly through the darkness. I retraced my steps, groping for the walls and thinking about the strange human voices I had heard. It was not long before I could tell that I had taken a path other than the route that had led me, so shortly before, close enough to the shore that the sound of the waves breaking was not the same echo that I could hear from my home, whenever the battles quieted down over in the war territory.

As I stooped to squeeze through an opening in the wall, I supposed that I had not gotten quite there. Then I perceived a faint glow, and with its help I was guided to the chamber where I had seen the girl in the jar. Good. Now I will be able to get out at Mar Jirjis, after I have stopped for a rest.

I lowered my bundle from my back and checked the dampness of the cloth. I sat down opposite the girl, inhaling deeply.

Why, as I stared at the amphora girl, did I feel such security? All of my anxiety and fear seemed to fade away. My breathing grew regular, my limbs relaxed, and a gentle, pleasant sleepiness rose to my head.

I looked at her. It seemed to me now that I had poorly estimated her age on the last occasion. She was not a girl. She was a small woman. A woman—as if she had aged in my absence; as if, in my absence, she had sat still in her small frame, waiting until my gaze would bring her to life, in her wholeness, sitting cross-legged before me. For me. In the shadowy obscurity of her young age, she had walked toward the light that is a woman's life, and was revealed now, reclaiming from time the shortening and shrinking of dimensions and bodies that its passage imposes.

And time also . . . in the short interval between my first visit and my second, the sap of time had run through her, the water of time . . . and now she reclaimed her soft flesh, as if for my eyes.

I look at her. I breathe deeply, but desire pounds at my heart like an enormous drum. The blood runs pulsing into my temples, and I can hear the pounding, so violent, in this profound silence.

I see Shamsa. I see Shamsa, the woman who has ripened. Shamsa has blossomed, and has abandoned her linen.

You have grown, Shamsa. You have grown so quickly that my hands can no longer manage. You have grown too fast for my fingers to keep up. Abandon your linen, Shamsa, and come now to velvet.

Shamsa laughed as she spread out her henna-red plaits of hair. She was not shy about her large body, which once had embarrassed her.

Her white flesh overflowed between my hands, in my arms. She grew and rose like blessed dough. Her thighs took on the fragrance of vanilla, her buttocks the taste of delicate biscuits. My saliva ran, distilled rose water.

I'm fat.

No. You are not fat. You are great, and profuse. You flow, abundant like divine grace when the heavens are pleased. Rounded like the peaches of Persia, sugary to the pits at their centers.

Shamsa laughs and her golden bracelets ring, and then so does my heart. The ringing rains down, a fine flour onto the snowy plains of her belly.

White ash above glowing coals—that is your skin, Shamsa. Tautened for me to see, showing itself to me. That I may blow a breath so light that it does not even ripple the velvet of ash or extinguish the hidden glow of the ember, lying in wait to ambush my skin, the palm of my hand, always cold. My mouth, hungry and thirsty and panting. Always.

I am fat, says Shamsa, because I have no country. I eat so that my body will grow, so that I can plant its weight firmly on the ground; so that my body will sense the earth there. We walked so much when we left our land that I was almost one with the air. Now I gain weight so that I may settle, so that I can feel the presence of a homeland. So that my dimensions will expand to occupy space. So that I can have some sort of solidity, whatever it may be, and alight in a home of my own.

Shamsa abandoned her linen when she abandoned her shame at the nakedness of her body, the nakedness of her movement through the light beneath my eyes. Shamsa forgot her shame when she began to learn velvet. At home, I tell her of it; I tell her velvet, all day long and until nightfall when she is supposed to return to her own family. But she learns it, too, in the lights of the night, and in its darkness, when heavy fighting makes it acceptable to her family that she stay at my home, even though the distance between the two homes is very short.

But I began to teach Shamsa velvet before the battles began. From the shop, I brought her the most beautiful velvet fabrics we had. Large swathes, which I would not reveal to her all at one time. Instead, for each one I told her a story—a velvet with every lesson—and she ascended with me in each level of pleasure, as the disciple of a Sufi master ascends, training her bliss through knowledge and disclosure, exercising her pleasure through discovery. Step by step, her senses became finer and she learned speech. She expressed her desire out loud, and demanded obedience and submission. She would teach me how to serve her senses and follow her way, in her body. Thus also she unlocked the bolts on her memory and told me who she was. She told me of her people, her family, and the land she had departed.

My father was very old when he crossed the river, Shamsa said. From the back of his worn-out mule that butted at the rocks in that impassable wilderness, he said to my mother, No. What you see is just an illusion. You are imagining it all, dreaming of the fogs of winter, the low clouds.

The country that we will reach is always green, but we are still outside of its merciful borders.

My father was forced to leave the rises of Kharbut and his tribe, the Hakkari, which in my grandfather's days was no longer well protected. We had become practically indistinguishable from the Ghamiri, the folk of the plains, whom we used to call the orphans or the dead cows. They had been our servants, our *riit*, not free herders like us.

My elderly father refused to let himself be named chief of our tribe by the Turks, which would mean paying the *jurak* on the *kabchur*, that is, a tax on the livestock. He refused to work as *ulam* or *bighar* for the state. He rejected sending men to work in forced labor gangs, and he refused the *dis kirazi*. He said no, we will not offer refuge, we will not feed passing troops against our will. We do not obey the soldiers' masters.

My grandfather, who loved my father more than any of his many other children, used to tell him—and to repeat to him—that with the Emir Amin Badirkhan, Sharif Pasha, and Abd al-Qadir Shamdinan, he founded the first Kurdish newspaper, to which they gave the title *Kurdistan*. They founded a school at the same time. The newspaper had to go underground and it repeatedly changed names, until they settled on *Hatawi Kurd*, which means 'The Kurdish Sun.' My mother told me these things, relating them from my father and thence my grandfather, the Sufi shaykh whose knowledge was so broad and deep. All of this was confirmed by my cousin, once a student. The war broke out. When the Turks entered, my grandfather and his comrades began to demand independence. At that, the Turks dedicated themselves to killing the Kurds. Whoever was left fled as far as they could when Mustafa Kemal Ataturk occupied Constantinople. They began to meet secretly, to prepare to proclaim their demand for independence. An English colonel in the British secret service made them optimistic promises. His name was Colonel Bill. But he was a liar. And from the Treaty of Paris with the Armenians to the Treaty of Lausanne, the Turks and the English fooled us, and we ended up as you see. I have preserved all of this, and more, in my memory.

We are not servants, says Hatawi, and I kiss the toes of both of her feet. But my grandfather did not like war and killing. And in the *rimal*, the large tent, when the revolutionary Shaykh Said al-Birani came to him with an offer that he and his tribe join the rebels, my grandfather refused. The conditions did not please him. He said that Shaykh al-Birani was rash and fickle, pushed by a desire for revenge and killing. His eyes, thought my grandfather, held a black harshness. And when—in the same *rimal*—there came to my grandfather the Aghri Dey, with a similar proposition, five years after that of Shaykh al-Birani, my grandfather took his time before answering. All of the great tribes were gathered to meet in the council. They discussed matters at length and drank tea. They went out and took care of their needs in the nearby grass and came back to talk more. They had dinner in uneasy silence and then placed before my grandfather a pair of slippers so that he would make a final decision for them, as was the custom. He put them on and went out of the council to the tent of his *bir*, the clan to which he belonged in the tribe. He spoke to them briefly, and the men nodded in agreement. They did not like unclean war, fighting that looks like *katchi,* that is, revenge. My grandfather slept that night, grieving, in his wife's embrace.

All of that happened before the revolt of Darsim, when the Turks hanged all the chiefs of the Kurdish tribes. But by then we were already far away, on other plateaus and heights. Even before the end of the *sin*— the mourning period—for his father, my father left, taking those who had stayed loyal to him, the men and their families. My father buried his father in Ghuristan, cutting a small hollow into the tombstone that he set above his father's grave so that birds could drink there and beg God's mercy for his father. On the grave marker my father drew the symbols he knew, as he had not learned to write well enough to engrave verses from the Qur'an. My father never did know how to read or write properly, even though his own father had been a student of Abu Muhammad Shanbaki, and one of the adherents of Abu al-Wafa al-Halawani, the first to obtain the title of Taj al-Arifin, Coronet of Those Who Know God. After studying at the Qur'an school of Kamiran Badirkhan, where he learned the Qur'an and the teachings of Islam in Kurdish, he learned the rudiments of Arabic as well. But his son—my father—never achieved anything close to his father's learning, because of the wars and revolts.

My father lay my grandfather in his grave and before the mourning period ended we were walking toward another land. The women hoisted the children and carried the light bundles that held their jewelry, the *bermirat* and *malwankat* to protect us from the evil eye. We followed the *diri,* we followed the fated path concealed for us in the distant skies, singing over and over in our hearts the old, sad chants of our Kurdish bards to the slow beat of the mules' hooves.

Your father was very unhappy, my mother told me. I would pass all of the other women in the caravan; I exhausted my mule to reach the front, to come near your father's mare. He could see me there, so near, and when he saw me he would turn his face away. He would not speak to me. My heart sank beneath my ribs, and I was perplexed to think of something I might do to lighten his sorrow, to tell him my love. I knew, when he refused to look in my direction, that I was forbidden to speak, to say anything, no matter what it might be. All that was left to me was song. So I sang to him, as I rode on near him, behind him, in a low voice:

From my earrings I will craft a horseshoe for his mount.
I will sever my precious bangles from my wrist,
And pound them into nails, into that nimble hoof.
From the braids of my long hair, I'll weave a bridle for his mount,
And there will never be one lovelier!
Ahh my heart, Tell him, and tell his horse, what I cannot give away
I hope he will be kind, perhaps relent and look my way . . .

For days we followed our fated path—we followed the *diri*, my mother told me—until we reached a merciful territory that seemed to welcome us and our animals. We lived there for years. It was a good life that granted us more than we could have hoped for, more than the pitiable servant of God deserves. That land held water, and bounty, herbs that our folk had never seen. Our clever, knowing grandmothers could not even name those plants or speak of their virtues. They advised us to be cautious and restrained with some of that land's vegetation. And then Shaykh Boldo came. My mother says "Shaykh Boldo," and then my cousin Fakhro, who studied in the schools of Beirut, interjects: His name is Shaykh Leopoldo Soldini, aunt. I read it in a book about our people that a French priest wrote. My mother smiles jokingly. Does the priest know the man's name better than he does himself? she asks Fakhro. We called him Shaykh Boldo and he answered with warmth. Tell that to your French priest, Fakhro, proud Mister Fakhro who studied in the schools of Beirut, dear Mister Fakhro of the grand stall in the vegetable market, who still has not even gotten married, to this very day . . . . Whatever the case, my mother continued, Shaykh Boldo came to us then, and lived among us until he was speaking our language. The plants that our clever grandmothers did not know, he told us, were not planted by the djinnis but by God, the All-Living, the Creator. Shaykh Boldo taught us how to use all of these plants as medicines, and we memorized his knowledge, all of it, before he left our land to die in Zakho, where he had gone, the first stage of his voyage back to his own faraway country in the lands of the Franks. In Zakho, to this day, there is a shrine to Shaykh Boldo visited by the sick. Invalids from everywhere, the sick of every faith, make pilgrimage to Shaykh Boldo's shrine. Many of them are cured through the merciful intercession of his pure soul.

Shamsa tells me that everything she knows and has taught me about the plants that she has often brought me, whenever she thought I needed one and judged it good for me, everything comes from the learning of Shaykh Boldo.

And Shamsa tells me that she is a knowing woman. I am not ignorant, she says, even if I did not go to the schools of Beirut. I know many things, on many subjects, that you do not know. And I am still learning, and I surprise you, do I not?

My mother tells me—says Shamsa—that we stayed in that land for many long and happy years, and it granted us more than the pitiable servant of God could hope for, and more than one could desire. Despite my father's strength and my mother's youth, and the preparation of dried mandragora that I will tell you about later, they had no children. But my father would not marry another woman, and his lack of offspring did not leave him miserable. He was happy and healthy in that high, faraway land, until one day he was visited by a Sufi of the Naqshbandi Order, who was on his way home after visiting his family in the highlands of Turkish Kurdistan. And like all travelers, the Naqshbandi had evening chat to spare, as he drank tea under a full summer moon.

The Naqshbandi said: Mawlana Khalid, who was a poor hermit from Qaradagh, from the tribe of Djaff, saw himself in a dream. On the road to the Holy Kaaba in Mecca, in this dream, he met a dervish in whose beard lice had nested. The dervish spent his days picking lice out of his beard and praying. The dervish said to Mawlana Khalid: Go without delay to a large city in the country of the Hindus called Delhi. Your salvation is there and you will never find it in any other place. Our master Khalid put on his slippers and walked. In Delhi he was easily led to the school of Shaykh Abdallah, despite the city's enormous size and population. It was as if an angel had taken his hand and guided him to the retreat, the tekiye of Shaykh Abdallah, who taught him the Way of the Naqshbandi Brethren. Shaykh Abdallah said to him: Return now to your country. Live in Sulaymaniye, and make adherents of your people. Teach them what you have learned.

The next day, the Naqshbandi traveler did not depart. He did not carry away the bundle that the women had prepared for him at dawn. My father prevented him from leaving, and he lived in our land for many days. Often, he and my father secluded themselves in the nearby plains.

After the Naqshbandi had gone, my father remained silent and dreamy for hours at a time—says my mother. Beneath his arm he carried a book that the voyager had left for him. It was called *The Enlightenment of Hearts*. My father—who did not read as well as he should have—would open it and place his hands upon its pages like a blind man, then shut it and put it under his pillow.

One evening my father told my mother that they would never be blessed with children if they did not leave that bounteous land, despite its riches. But first he must travel to Arbil to visit the grave of the last of the Sufis, Shaykh Amin the Kurd, the Naqshbandi, of the Shafi'i school of Islamic jurisprudence, and author of *The Enlightenment of Hearts*. He would illuminate my father's heart, and then my father would be able to read at once, though he had none of the learning of the schools. The Shaykh would guide him to the land where he must dwell, so that the killing and the evil of the soldiers would not reach him, and so that God would bless him with sound offspring.

By day my father fasted and prayed, and by night he stayed away from my mother, before journeying to Arbil alone. My mother sang her sad *mawwal* to him, weeping, as he fastened the saddle and his sparse provisions upon his horse. All evening she cried hard in the arms of her aged mother-in-law, who had lived more than one hundred years and had lost her vision. It is the *biri* who took him, mother . . . . The djinni women of the springs have stolen him from me and he will not return . . . . The ancient woman stroked my mother's hair and told her stories, the fantastic and strange tales of faithful lovers, until she fell asleep in the old woman's arms, just like a child.

In the ewes' birthing season my father returned. Only my mother recognized his form from afar. She shouted. Yes, it is his horse—look, it's him, my man! She took off her shoes, threw her wrap over her head, picked up the water jug and ran to him. She grabbed the bridle, led the exhausted horse to its watering trough in front of the tent, and helped the exhausted rider to dismount, slowly and carefully, as if he were ill. She put her arm around his waist and his arm around her neck and supported his body against her hip, as if his tired bones were dislocated. Silently, the men remained outside, watching. The women averted their attention. They did not run to heat water until my mother had shouted to them from inside the tent.

The next day, no one asked my mother why she had not cut her husband's hair or shaved his long beard before she bathed him and dressed him in clean clothes. They visited him every day but in the beginning not even the eldest dared to put any questions to him. One day, though, the elder addressed him, after clearing his throat hard: Shaykh of our tribe, a human being is not a *mara azman*, a serpent of the sky, who can change its color and form at will. Shaykh of our people, a person is not a chameleon. A person has something of Our Lord's wisdom, and a chameleon does not. And the will of God—Great is He—contains that which we cannot understand or even apprehend.

After a long silence my father replied, clearing his throat hard too. God, Exalted is He, wishes us, according to His will, to understand and apprehend fully. If we wish it, we may open our eyes and we will see. We will see everything, and we will see Him around us in what He hath made.

There was a long and profound silence: the men could hear the ewes bleating from the far pastures. My father spoke again. Know that for me, the entire world is nothing but a mirror. And know that in every speck blaze thousands of suns. If you were to pierce the heart of a single drop of water, from it would fall water enough to fill an ocean. Examine every grain of sand and you will find hundreds of human beings within. The tiny insect possesses as many legs as does the great elephant. And a drop of rain has all of the attributes of the torrential Nile River. The core of a grain of wheat is akin to the yield of a hundred harvests, and in a kernel of maize is concealed a world, entire and complete. Every thing, and every question, is a point on the circle of the present. From every point in this ring emerge thousands of forms. Every point in its own orbit is at once a circle and a sphere that rotates . . . and the world is a mirror to the world.

The bleating of the sheep echoed across the still air of the tent, until the eldest cleared his throat and spoke in a shaking voice. Shaykh of our folk, we know but little; and your knowledge is too vast for our threadbare turbans.

It is not my knowledge, said my father. My words are but a mirror of the mirror of Shaykh Mahmud Shabastari, the blessed Persian.

Relate to us more of his knowledge that you learned in Arbil, in the quarters of the people who know God. Perhaps God, Exalted is He, will have mercy on us and treat us gently, said the eldest. We are only shepherds of livestock, and few of us know how to read.

What I learned in Arbil was not how to read well, or how to puzzle out the shapes of letters. But you are here before me, yet you do not hear what I tell you, even though I do not write it and compel you to unravel my letters.

Surely it is because we learn through storytelling and proverbs, said the eldest. And our children do not thus rebuke us as if we have closed minds.

Listen, then, said my father. Listen to some of what I heard from those who guided me, in my absence from you.

The ewes and lambs had stopped bleating and were now asleep in their enclosure. Nothing disturbed the men's heavy silence but the sound of wood popping under the pots of soup. Sitting in their capacious tent, they could not hear my mother's low sobbing in her mother-in-law's embrace. It is the Naqshbandi, elderly mother. He stole away my man when he spent that summer in our land. It is the evil Naqshbandi.

Now you know that we must go, my father said to my mother a few months later. Not because of what the men of the tribe repeat about me, for they are ignorant and their hearts are closed. With them my knowledge is of no use. We must go for the sake of traveling to that blessed, promised land that is always green and lies along the water. For it was confirmed to me, as I was in the presence of the soul of the felicitous Shafi'i Shaykh who enlightened my heart: a great evil has assembled in this land. Here we will never see sound offspring or felicity. That promised land is not an illusory promise. Only a very few men will leave with us, when the moon grows full. We will carry our belongings and my elderly mother on a single mule, and behind us we will lead half of our share of the head of livestock, leaving the other half behind as compensation for our departure.

My mother did not dare to speak or protest. She knew that my father would not stand for long what the people of the tribe were saying of him. He would not endure their insinuations that with his new knowledge he had become one of the infidel Yazdis, worshipers of the Devil and of Fire; or that, at best, he was among those who had turned to Shi'ism, elevated the imam Ali to the status of prophet, and called themselves People of the Truth. Those Yazdis had a chief, Mubarak Shah, Baba Khushin, whom they followed as he strayed afar, as far as the land of Iraq. He lived in sin with a woman whom he had not married, and took her along with his six male disciple companions, to live among them—and it was said that she 'lived with' all of them. Her name was Fatima Ud al-Ban, or Bibi Fatima, and she was the sister of the famous poet Baba Tahir al-Hamdan, who tried neither to return her to the right path nor to kill her. Hearing all of that from the women, my mother did not dare to speak or to voice any objection to following the illusions of these prophecies. She knew, too, that a woman must not oppose the words of her man if he is in a weak position in his tribe. So how could she do so now when the tribe itself had splintered and weakened?

My mother bathed her mother-in-law, swathed her like a nursing infant, and stopped weeping. The night before their departure she slept in the arms of my father, telling him droll stories, the ones that had made him laugh loudly in former times, and she sang to him and kissed his hands and the gemstones in his silver ring until sleep took him, a smile on his lips. At dawn the next day, my father kissed the hands of the eldest of the tribe and embraced the other men's shoulders. He gave his mount a kick and led his little caravan away. He did not turn around once, nor did my mother. He did not look her in the face before they reached the plains and then crossed the river to the promised land that is always green and lies along the sea.

Sad—your story is sad, pretty Hatawi.

No, said Shamsa. My story is not sad, because I am not in that part of my family's story that I am telling you. Now I know that I am elsewhere, in another story that comes before the one I have told, saddening you with its ending. For after you taught me the velvet and told me its story, in which I am—as the travelers and French voyagers saw me—an ignorant slave, who swaggers in the splendor of her velvet, the splendor of my skin, glistening with the ferociousness of its appetite like the savage fur of wild felines, I will tell you where my gentle force is hidden, where my fierce gentleness lies. I say "my velvet," for I am that velvet palm gloving a hand of iron, that expression that suits me . . . .

Tell, lovely Hatawi, I said to Shamsa.

That is not my name. I am not Hatawi, and I am not Shamsa. I am Suryash. The Sun, in the language of my ancestors, the Kassites, descendants of the djinnis.

I am the djinni Suryash. I am granddaughter of one of the beauties for whom King Solomon sent westward. Four hundred maidens, the most beautiful of God's creatures, to fulfil the royal yearnings of Solomon. Four hundred virgins, to answer his majestic restiveness, for he had only to pass through his harem to feel an aversion to the women he kept there. God had granted him wisdom and knowledge such that to know a woman to the core he had merely to gaze at her; and before she could undress in his private quarters his desire would abandon him. And at that she would begin to droop and sag though she was yet a young bud of a girl, her breasts swelling. She would enfold herself in that fragrance of her own that now she would never diffuse, in that royal neglect. For the king devoted himself to women from afar who came to him boxed in his dreams like precious gifts that never truly arrive and are never deflowered.

Four hundred maidens, the most beautiful of God's creatures. So beautiful were those maidens that they woke the djinnis inside the earth as their virginal caravan passed above. Thus awoke four hundred male djinnis who were under the command of the demon Djazad. They requested their lord's permission to intercept the lovelies on their way overhead to the harem of King Solomon. In his consuming jealousy of the favor the wise king enjoyed with the Creator, Djazad allowed them even more. Taking the form of handsome princes who flaunted the most precious of garments and recited the loveliest of verses, they bewitched the hearts of the maidens, who promptly slid off their mounts. Those maidens spent the night loving the youths and when dawn came they found themselves naked and alone in the desert.

When they arrived at the palace and stood in the presence of Solomon, the king could see into their innermost selves. And thus he saw that they were no longer virgins. And because they were no longer fit for him, he repulsed—*karada*—the young women and the fruit of their wombs to the deserted steppes. There, their bellies grew large and they gave birth to Kurds—'the repulsed.'

Yet the Kurds did not get their name from King Solomon's rejection of their mothers. They got their name because, in the Persian tongue, *kurd* means 'the brave hero.' It is said that the origin of the word, before its corruption across the years, was *kargh,* meaning 'wolf,' or perhaps 'wild cat' . . . the creature who is covered in velvet fur, and who thus resembles me.

I will tell you, too, that it was the women who led the Kurdish attacks on Sargon of Akkad, who shook with fear whenever he heard a Kurdish expression. For Sargon of Akkad knew, from the tales of his ancestors, that we were the children of the princely djinnis, raised by those strong women who lived alone in the steppes before ascending the rocky heights, neighbors to the djinnis from Urama to Mount Judi . . . there, where Noah's ark stopped at the end of its wanderings. There, where the ship of Gilgamesh anchored, on the summit of Mount Nizir, like a paper hat.

Djinnis or wolves or wild cats—because we are strong and fierce and bold, sending terror into the hearts of anyone who gives us reason to fear for our freedom. But we do not like war or mortal combat. After my Kassite ancestors attacked the children of Hammurabi, they entered Babel peacefully and ruled it for ten centuries. Gradually they renounced rule, living on there as construction workers, stablemen, and artisans who taught the pharaohs' laborers many things. For so long they lived in peace that they forgot the first things about fighting, and so the wily Assyrians attacked them. Crushing the Kassites, they swarmed over their territory. They plundered and enslaved the men and abused the women. But there emerged among the Assyrians Sargon the Second, builder of Khorsabad, who freed the Kassites and marched with them to the Khabor, a tributary of the Euphrates. There on the wide banks they remembered who they were. They regained their courage, their passion for freedom. They became herders; they perfected the use of weapons and the arts of fighting, and were the first to think of using flaming arrows to send fright into the heart of anyone who approached too boldly.

Since the destruction of Nineveh more than six hundred years before the birth of the Messiah, we have worshiped horses, Suryash, the Prophet Muhammad, and our freedom wherever we may be on this earth on which there is no earth for us. Ever since the djinnis knew our mothers, as they made their way toward the wise King Solomon, and to this day, to this year—the Kurdish year 2587—we reside in our courage and freedom, in our solitude and in our free flight over lands owned by others, across borders barb-wired by identity papers and soldiers. So how can we be your servants, my master? How can we be your servants? asked Suryash Hatawi Shamsa, radiant in her pealing laugh.

Repeat the story of the velvet to me, she said. I would love to hear it again before I move you on, and you move me on. On, to another lesson

. . . .

How could one possibly describe that day!

My nights were interrupted by the huge aircraft carrier that had anchored to the south. It stayed for days and days, and fired its balls of flame at the low mountains opposite the coast. Flocks of rapid, nervous airplanes took off and landed endlessly, and the sky above my head was a theater of resounding explosions. Even the rain came down gray, so that I could not even benefit by collecting and storing it. Later, I was forced to clean out all of my large pots. Their interiors had gone black.

But that particular day seemed divinely ordered in its astonishing beauty. I told myself that perhaps my reaction was a matter of my long stay inside, for I had not left my home except to go out on my verandah. Perhaps it was that which gave me to see in the exploding springtime beauty a joy that I could barely endure. I walked—along the reeds and maize that I had planted between my house and the ocean—all the way to the seashore. I was convinced that the carrier was no longer there, despite the continuing explosions, which had receded somewhat into the distance. I saw a broad and calm expanse of sea, so intensely alight that its blue color appeared golden: it was an enormous plain of gold, a plain on which all colors blazed at once.

The sight so dazzled my eyes that I could no longer make out the horizon, nor the fine line marking where dry land began. So when I saw flames at one end of the Avenue des Français, I thought it was the fanciful product of my overwhelmed vision. I closed my eyes and wrapped my head in the cloth that I used as my pack, now empty. When I looked again, I was certain that what I saw really was fire. I sprinted back to my house, screaming deliriously. My plan was to acquire a light for the oil lamp wick that I had prepared long before in hopes of just such a coincidence, one that would make my felicity complete by offering fire and light.

Before I turned into my street I saw him. Just like that, opposite me, staring at me, planting his legs stolidly in the ground, firm and unmoving. He was tensed, ready to spring, his coat of short white hair gleaming under the strong columnar rays of the sun. He was alone. I had heard no barking. I had not seen the rest of the pack. There was no tree nearby, no strong, tall trunk that I could climb. I did not run, for if I were to run he would simply chase me. That had happened to me once as a boy. I remembered also that the sight of an upright man can arouse fright and animosity in wild animals. I dropped to the ground, supporting myself on my hands and knees, and began to crawl backward, staying on my hands and knees until I disappeared from his sight. I listened to find out whether he was following me but I heard nothing suspicious.

Whatever the situation, my only recourse was to get to that fire, somewhere near the end of Avenue des Français. I could not decide: should I head straight across the concretions of collapsing buildings, climbing over whatever blocked my path, or should I run along the seashore, where I could see across the level, unoccupied ground and be safe from surprise but would be within range of his quick legs and his jaws?

I decided in favor of the seafront for several reasons. First, I needed to get a clearer idea of the fire's precise position so that I could reach it by the quickest possible route; and second, in the worst of conditions, and even if an entire pack came after me, I could throw myself into the water and stay there until boredom or despair beat them back, or until they forgot that I was a land creature who would be good prey.

That is what I did, and he did not catch up with me. I saw no trace of him. The source of the fire was the framing beneath the roof tiles of an old house. It was still smoldering even though nothing remained but some heavy pillars and beams. In a few hours' time it would probably have gone completely to ashes.

It was not easy to reach the fiery wood. I walked a short distance away from the house of the roof tiles and found a plank that might have plummeted from that very house when it blew up before exploding into flames. I thrust it into the nearest embers until it took flame, whereupon I started back along my return route, carrying my torch and feeling tremendously happy. I was heedless of the wild dogs, or even of wolves if that is what they were, as long as I held in my hand something with which I could defend myself and face any danger that I might encounter.

I reached my verandah. If anyone had been listening to the wild sounds I was making he would have thought me completely insane. I leveled the wick of my lamp and straightened the braided end so that it sat properly, soaked it thoroughly in oil, and lit it. I jumped up and down like an ape—what, I said, could possibly trouble me from this point on? Even if the olive oil runs out, any fat will work, animal or vegetable, not to mention the castor-oil plant or a date palm: pressing the fruit would yield as much oil as I could possibly need. When the fat floats to the surface of their nectar, I can collect it in any fine-weave cloth and store it in one of any number of containers. Who or what would dare to come near to my house or to me from now on, when I have fire?

For long hours I sat watching the wick burn. In the evening I carried my wool blanket out to the stone bench on my veranda, and after I had surrounded the lamp with a metal can to protect it from gusts of wind, I stretched out among my flowering plants and roses, eating a lettuce shoot that was so sweet it seemed to have acquired a dusting of powdered sugar. I began to envisage the smell of roasting that I would soon enjoy. I imagined the skin of a grilled fish on my thin tin plate, the slowly melting fat from the backsides of plump birds, the warm, pure, trickling oil from the fat upper legs of frogs that I would waylay in the pond near Parliament Square, and the low popping of olive oil as I fried those appetizing white mushrooms that certainly must have pushed their way up through the crannies in the goldsmiths' souq after the last rains of winter.

All of these pleasures Shamsa had taught me. It was Shamsa who trained my taste buds so finely. She used to tell me that fat is the blessing we are offered by the creatures that the Lord made it lawful for us to eat. It is not nature's garbage, as my mother used to call it. Fat is our bodies' temperature regulator, and it preserves us from the attacks of the world outside. Through fat a woman amasses her reserves, ready to cradle her fetus in her basin of pearly flesh; and fat inheres in the liquid of testicles that yields strong male offspring. Is it not blood sacrifice and fats consumed by fire whose fumes and vapors we have been sending to placate the gods since early times?

That was in the ages of the ancients, Shamsa. Fat harms men's hearts, I tell her. No, she responds, laughing; and her fat, blessed and resplendent, shakes beneath my eyes and nose. Why does your mother burn oil before the Virgin Mary's image every Saturday evening? Isn't it really smoldering fat that she is offering to her intercessor as a plea for mercy? What's more, fat does not harm men's hearts unless it is combined with sugar. Eat as much oil and fat as you wish, but do not follow them with a sweet. Wait two or three hours, and then eat a piece of fruit or a sweet. That is all there is to it. Fat is a blessing.

And now, open your mouth. Do not chew so quickly. Close your eyes. Leave the fat to melt and fill your mouth before you pitch it into your stomach, scorning it in your ignorance. Give it to me with your tongue: from your mouth to mine, give me a morsel of what you have chewed, what your mouth has already worked into liquid. We will eat together as if we have a single mouth. Take your hands from my hips and let the enjoyment of taste linger in your mouth alone. Turn out the light and come, let us eat together. Come, we will eat each other. Eat of my body.

My heart aches in my chest when I want you this badly, Shamsa. When your body fills every organ of mine, and bears down so much that it hurts.

When I opened my eyes to distance Shamsa even slightly from my memory I saw him. He held the same position, about ten meters away. Planting his legs in the ground, rigid and motionless, he was staring right at me.

O God.

With two leaps I reached the opening to the lower level. I dove and slammed the metal door down over my head.

Ass. What an ass I am. With two ears as long as date-palm fronds. So—I will protect myself with fire? How could I have found that believable? Did my small, slow mind think—just for instance—that the dog would stand still, patiently waiting until I picked up my length of timber, held it over the lamp wick until it was well on fire, and then attacked him, waving my homemade torch to frighten him into running away?

Ass, God, how stupid I am. How slow-witted could I be? I went on muttering, shifting restlessly in my spot. For more than an hour he stayed right outside, howling, and then he let loose with prolonged, wolf-like cries that terrified me and made my flesh crawl. Several times I got up to peer from the little openings that I had made in the stone of my veranda, that is, in the roof of my home, sealing them with shards of thick glass that I had brought home from the Mosque of Mansur Assaf and the Patisserie Hallab so that I could bring the daylight inside. Of course, now I could see nothing. Concentrating on the lamp that sat somewhere above my head, in an attempt to reassure myself, I reminded myself over and over that I had not heard any sound of destruction or of things being broken.

He was still up there, howling. He stood still for a few moments, and then prowled around the veranda and in the street alongside my garden before returning to his long dirges, and I went back to scolding myself harshly as I took some firm decisions that I would begin to implement the next day at dawn. My first resolution was to fortify my surrounding hedge with a heavy metal cable. The second was to light a permanent fire in a deep hollow or the like that I could dig at the edge of the veranda. But the hedge would never be high enough to prevent him from jumping over it unless I redid it entirely, and who could guarantee that I could finish it before the beast returned? And to keep a fire eternally burning was no easy solution. I would have to roam far to gather the necessary wood and kindling.

O God, O God. I will never get out of this place. I will stay hidden for a week or more until he forgets about me, gets bored, despairs of my coming out. Then he will know that I am cleverer than he is, far cleverer, and that he will not be able to get the best of me.

In my mind I summoned back the exceptional beauty of that day. It had been more splendid than it ought to have been, I told myself, too intensely beautiful for the Creator to permit its enjoyment to one of His creatures. It had been the sort of pleasure that exceeds lawful measure and thereby obligates the Lord's creature to pay the price. Whenever my mother laughed hard, she would implore her Lord's pardon and seek absolution. God be merciful, she would say; permit me the favor of this abundant laughter. And if it were a Friday—the day of the Messiah's crucifixion and passion—she forbade herself outright to laugh. This is inappropriate, she would say angrily. Today is Friday. Lord, do not hold me responsible . . . .

I began to summon back the extraordinary loveliness of this day whose pleasure and joys I had been forbidden to fully know. I pondered the retribution that God had brought down on me in return for all that had happened: the retribution that bayed above my head.

It was a day like unto the day in which those two American pilots were told: Do not release the atomic bomb 'Little Boy' (my father would say mockingly to the father of our neighbor Abd al-Karim) unless the weather is fine and bright, and the sky perfectly blue, unspoiled by even a single cloud.

Why, Hajj? Abu Abd al-Karim would ask my erudite father, with a pleasure that compensated for the poor state of business in the souq.

Because, replied my father, proud of his knowledge, what the Americans really wanted was to test the destructive capabilities of the bomb, which had just been made, not to win the war as they said. The Japanese did not have even a single state-of-the-art airplane able to circle high enough in the sky. The Japanese wanted to surrender, but the Americans delayed their acceptance so that they could test their bomb, and also to needle the allies, especially Stalin.

To needle the allies? asked Abu Abd al-Karim. How do you mean, Hajj?

Of course, said my father, his pride at his own intelligence obviously mounting. Of course, to needle the allies. They had reached the stage of dividing the booty, the postwar stage. Each wanted to show his neighbor that he was the strongest and so should get the lion's share of the spoils and also should take over the decision-making about leadership and power. And in particular to spite Stalin, twirling his moustaches as he dreamed of the Red Army spreading as far as our lands.

To hell with them—Stalin, and the reds, and communism, said Abu Abd al-Karim.

It was a day, no doubt, just like that one had been. And then, this day had been enhanced by the thousands of suns that flamed upward in a single moment . . . the largest of rainbows, fluid with millions of colors . . . much like the moment, surely, in which the Lord created heaven and earth. And then, black rain on steaming corpses . . . .

And there was the sinking of the Titanic. Though it was the strongest and largest steamship in the world, it went down—only because the weather was gorgeous, a night shimmering with stars, an ocean quietly submissive to the vast ship's oil, the air still in its black hull. Humanity oblivious, distracted by play, confident (in the grace and glory of its mastery) of the order and stability of things. That is when the Lord launches His fatal blow. He raises you to the most sublime of heights to dash you low, to smite you against the earth. That is when you receive the blow to end all blows.

What can I do now, Shamsa, with the wrath of the Lord? The Lord's wrath that He hath shown to me: what can I do with it when I am engulfed by you?

Come back to me, said Shamsa. Take off your clothes and lie down in the velvet, that we may wrap ourselves completely in it. Lie down, that you may find me once again within you, and that you may bring me back to you. Let your skin press against mine, pore against pore, tissue to tissue, that the nap may rise between warp and weft, as if, at the first touch, I am quivering already.

Come back to me, and teach me velvet. Tell me how fully I have become velvet.

Velvet, Shamsa, is the third dimension of cloth—or the fabric in three dimensions whose achievement perplexed humanity until only a few centuries ago. How do you emulate a petal? How do you imitate the inside of the rose, the interior of a flower's corolla? How do you reproduce this final chapter of the beauty of living things? The crafting of velvet—once it was known—was considered humanity's finest innovation in the search for more beautiful fabric. The astonishment it generated was as great as the achievement was simple. All it required was two warps. Between them, the weaver inserts a stick to raise the second layer above the first. That primary warp is woven densely to create a strong backing. The raised warp is cut or shaved to form the velvet nap.

That is how carpet emerged from the woven wool rug.

And that is how the weaver's appetite for play and imagination was whetted. Instead of a single stick, why not use two, to insert shapes, designs, and stripes, whether monochrome or in a different tone, and by different and varied knottings of the filament. And the plush, whose beauty you glory in on the *yalik* that you wear, is made by introducing velvet onto raw silk, sovereign of light and shadow playing on the same color, offering an even richer exercise of the imagination, and still more lights and shadows. The heights of this artistry were reached when from the loom streamed three thousand two hundred bobbins of thread, each weighted by a leaden marble—in place of the sticks, of course. At such a loom, a weaver would not complete more than four small centimeters in an entire day's work.

Raw silk comes from this earth, Shamsa, and likewise the first specimens of velvet: from the carpets of the Persians, as you said, to Ottoman Anatolia. And until the invasion of the Mongols, attacking at the command of their leader Timurlane, the most beautiful fabrics remained those made in Syria and Anatolia. They were sent throughout the world, but of the sovereigns and lords who received them, none could fathom their mysteries.

Why? Beginning hundreds of years before the birth of the Messiah, and from Sassanian Persia to Byzantine and then Muslim Syria, the secretary of the guild of drapers and weavers was the sole possessor of the designs, the only one who could calibrate the dyestuff and calculate the number of knots in a weave; and he led his team as a ship's chief rower leads his oarsmen. He alone knows where it is going, and knows the thread of its passage. He alone has memorized the secret behind the cloak of the Persian King of Kings, for example, and how and when the sun or the winged bull should ascend there. It was he who had perfect command of the mathematics required to figure out and engineer and control the infinity of design and line.

The weavers of Syria were kept under close surveillance by means of spies, who hemmed them in as assiduously as they did the craftsmen who stamped and printed currency. Indeed, for long stretches of history their precious fabric was considered government property—until the ninth century. The surveillance system was so stifling that Byzantium's weavers began to flee to Persia or to sell their knowledge to the great powers, if they did not find themselves prisoners of those powers after Zenobia had lost her war and the Sassanian Ardeshir I occupied Antioch.

But I will return to the tale of the weaver later.

In a word, it was Mehmet the Conqueror, seventh sultan–caliph of the Ottoman Empire, who opened the eyes of the West and schooled lusty European appetites when he conquered Constantinople in the mid-fifteenth century. His sublime taste and his splendid garments dazzled the lords of the West to the point that one of their master artists clothed the saint Mar Jirjis—St. George, or Khidr as the Muslims call him—in Ottoman fashion, as if he were a high official of the Sublime Porte. As for the velvet garments of Sulayman the Legislator, they choked the folk of Vienna with envy more dangerously even than did the long and griev-

ous siege of the city, beneath the rain that fell from the Austrian sky. The Conqueror was so magnificent, as splendid and suffocating as his velvets, depositing a resentful covetousness in the heart, that his winter departure from the chill ramparts left behind a sort of regret, akin to the sorrow in a woman's heart when she spurns her lover only to find him submit to her rejection and bid her farewell. With the seeds of desire tunneling deep in their entrails, artists in the West embarked on their desperate attempts. They filled the pages of their sketchbooks in defiant response to the reflection of the light rippling along the nap, trying to corral its richness. Sulayman the Magnificent entered from the most beautiful gate ever opened in a wall. And he stayed there, in the blazing imagination, in the pages of the earliest translations of *The Thousand and One Nights*. For the velvet etched richly in deep and dappled hues was embroidered with the smoke curling from the narghileh's tobacco and the cardamom wafting from the breasts of young women, yielding to the vapors of yearning. It pervaded the writings of the philosophers of the Age of Light as they saluted the grand luxury of liberty. It infused music inspired by the serail of the East and the rustle of its fabrics that alone intimated how the ear might be captivated by the raucous swish of velvet. When the velvet of the Muslim was no longer a source of terror, awestruck travelers voyaged to countries in which threads of gold mingled with velvet, setting fire to their imaginations as did the suns setting over those lands. Napoleon himself would don his imperial velvet for his coronation. Catching the fever of the Orient, poets would receive their listeners seated in poses that placed them somewhere along the banks of the Bosphorus.

All of this velvet—you hover behind it all, Shamsa. Your likeness: the image of a woman replete with the grace of her overflowing body. The shrewd and seductive woman, profligate and perilous, censored, prohibited, dreamed of through vaporous fogs, in the trembling of desires guarded by eunuch militias, repressed like the voices of women: languid, somnolent, conspiring, surreptitious.

Ohh . . . all of that?

And more, Shamsa . . .. Castration menaces me when I come near you, since I am the phantasms of my own desires and my imagination has had to play like the darting wind in deserted town squares to salvage my weak and flagging parts. And because the velvety skin of the peaches could implant needles and thorns that might well inflame and ulcerate my skin. Does this not happen often to God's creatures?

Yes, says Shamsa, laughing. Finish the story.

This is a story that one does not finish, Shamsa, but it might be disrupted, and grievously so.

The Doge of Venice—for the city had inherited Constantinople's primacy in the domain of velvet and gold embroidery—gazed down upon St. Mark's Square, garbed in the velvet habit that was the sign of his official and established dominion. He gazed at the standards of the city's powerful families, fluttering atop palaces and hanging from windows, fashioned and brocaded in the material that was the very symbol of Venice's florescence and superiority over kingdoms. That is, in velvet.

He gazed down upon it all as he proclaimed the start of the six-month period in which the city's inhabitants would don their masks to deliberate on the city's politics—a secret politics shot through with murky conspiracy. During that time the politicians would put on their velvet robes whenever they were to pass through the streets so that onlookers would recognize them as members of the elite and would mind their behavior accordingly, preserving status hierarchy.

But before velvet's insurgence and its arrogance were crushed, before velvet became corduroy in fabric's age of decadence, announcing the rise of democracy, the end of the age of privilege, and the era of slaves toiling inside gloomy factories, as my father would say . . . . Before that time, velvet was able to preserve the nobility of tradition. For as the elite of the countryside began to grow wealthy and to recognize their wealth, they realized their power to confront the oppression that urban societies had been able to visit on them. Before the lamentable downfall of the Ottoman Empire, to possess a velvet garment was to possess the sign of entrée to full adult life. Your grandmother's *yalik*, her vest embroidered with threads of silver and embellished with buttons, was a necessity for any trousseau, as it was a symbol of a man's power and superiority and of a woman's sexual maturity and her readiness to obey.

How can you say obedience and sexual maturity in the same breath? exclaims Shamsa. Is that how you can say that I have become velvet? And the shrewd and seductive woman, profligate and perilous, censored, prohibited, dreamed of through vaporous fogs?

They are one and the same, Shamsa. She obeys only her desires, and it is her lusts that strengthen a man's body, that he may surmount himself, not his woman. Mount her, that her desire may mount to the summit she desires, summit of the sky to which she raises him.

Woman of velvet, you must never come to a halt before the apparent meaning of words; you must never stop at the outer skin of things.

You have completed it, now, petal of the corolla. You have completed your learning, and perfected your body, and your femininity. And beyond completion lies only the anguish that is felt and the anguish that is inflicted, and the ever more complex obscurity of what comes between presence and absence. Nothing but lace . . . and the agony in my heart.

Nothing could extract me from my burrow. Nothing but hunger.

I will not die here, I told myself.

The more I postponed my exit, though, the more feeble I became. And the stronger the beast I faced grew.

I decided not to be absent for long. Only long enough to make a spear or something of that sort, a weapon I could use to fend him off if he attacked me. If he were with his pack, of course, it would all be over in a few moments. A matter of minutes, and I would no longer feel anything.

I went outside, as far as the veranda. The lamp was still flaring and I hurried to fill it with oil. Before making my way through the garden, I let out some cries to test whether he was close by. I did not hear him howling, nor could I hear the others. I sensed nothing suspicious but I stayed for a time where I was: perhaps he was laying a trap for me. He would get me to come out of my territory, confident of my safety, and then would lure me onto his terrain. No doubt he had marked it out with his urine, patrolling its air with his powerful nostrils.

I dropped to all fours, trying—with due caution—to smell a trace of his pee, but in vain. I wanted to learn whether he considered prowling in my area to be part of his own territorial rounds or whether he thought of this as alien ground.

I retreated hastily to the garden. I was so nervous that I could not swallow the one small wild red tomato that I picked from a wilting stem. I moved between the furrows, watering them even though it was not the proper time to water, in the heat of the midday sun.

Then an enchanting idea came to me. I filled my stomach with water and sat waiting for it to reach my bladder. When I could feel it accumulating, I picked up my stick and tied my homemade rucksack around me. I took my departure from Souq Ayas, going out to Rue Allenby and then to Rue Weygand and on to the high end of Avenue Foch. I passed in front of the shwarma shops near the establishment of Théophile Khoury, but I gave up any thought of searching their interiors for a knife or other sharp implement that I could fasten to the end of my stick, for I could already see that these eateries, exposed to the street, were completely bare. I pressed on until I reached the Rivoli, continuing what I had begun at my verandah, that is, peeing a few drops every twenty or thirty steps. It was not easy to do, and so instead of turning to climb toward Ahdab Parking, the Café Parisiana, and then the Metropole, I decided—on the basis of how much remaining urine I estimated I had—to return quickly by way of Rue de Byblos to Rue Samadi, Rue Abdallah Bayham, and then to Rue Fakhri Bek, Rue de Tripoli, and home. Thus I would have tried at least— and as an experiment—to define a circle that would be my own territory. I would see whether he entered it, and whether we were capable, the two of us, of finding some sort of accord, a possible symbolic code by which we could begin our coexistence peacefully in this, God's wide world.

But before I turned in the direction of Cinema Byblos I saw them. He was at the head of the pack but he held himself apart from the group, a few meters distant. They were crossing the entire length of Place des Martyrs. They stopped before the police building, where they huddled together, peering in all directions. I hid behind some scattered plywood boards that had fallen from the billing of the film *The Lovers*, still in fragments above my head. I began to watch them. I told myself that if they moved toward me I would run like the wind.

They were swiveling their heads in every direction and sniffing the air. Surely, I thought, they were catching the scent of my urine. It must have reached them, with the wind coming from the east, from the sea, behind me . . . and so they would decide not to head in my direction, understanding that this piece of land was occupied, that it had a master.

There were more of them than I had seen—or thought I had seen—the night of my fever, as they devoured their human prey in the little souqs in the vicinity of Maarad. All were about the same size, that of mature wolves, to judge by what I had seen on television or heard about these creatures. Congregated in this way in front of the headquarters of the Security Bureau, hardly moving, they looked very much like the ordinary dogs that wander the streets of poor quarters, massing around butcher shops and avoiding the cruelty of children who persecute and torment them.

As I watched, it dawned on me that I no longer feared them. I even thought about coming out from my hiding place behind the thin boards and making some sort of commotion to see what they would do. The way they were crowding together, and the fact that I could now plainly see them, enhanced my dawning sense of courage and capability even in light of their number. The feeling led me to imagine myself boldly stepping forth, my body perfectly erect, and walking toward them with a firm step as I had seen film heroes do. Who knows, I said to myself, maybe they would react by running away. In some corner of their memory must linger a residue of images that remind them of humans' undoubted dominion over them, images of their submission and obedience to us. And anyway, who said that the upright human form arouses the animosity of wild animals? That might be true of large animals. But I'm bigger than a dog.

Suddenly they moved, in one simultaneous shudder, choreographed like a school of fish, as if something—an electric wave—had shot through the air and hit them all at once. I froze, crouching in my hiding place, trying to restore my regular breathing. They began running behind him toward the Parisiana, then turned together so precisely it was as if they were a single body—running directly toward me and the Tripoli service taxi stop at Ahdab.

Before I could begin to run I saw them swerve at the Mutanabbi Building and the tinsmiths' souq. Though they disappeared from my sight completely I stayed exactly where I was, my limbs paralyzed. I congratulated myself on preserving my safety, sarcastically invoking my 'pea brain,' which is exactly how my mother—God's mercy upon her soul— used to describe me. How could I have possibly thought that I might frighten them? Bigger than a dog—so that was me? And their number? Two lions can seize a bull the size of a truck. The traces of awareness about human superiority in their memory? Dog memory? *Ya ayn*, what an ass I was. Most of these dogs were born here and had never seen a human being or even the shadow of one . . . and what about the man they took as prey under my nose in the small souqs near Maarad? *Ya ayn*. God keep my mother and let her dwell in His vast gardens of paradise.

My mother used to say that Nasser's brain was the size of a pea. My father would shake his head sadly and make no comment, and so my mother would forge ahead. The Israelis, she would say, convinced him that they were going to come from the east, and so he lay in wait to the west—or the other way around, I don't remember now, but it isn't important, anyway. The pea-brain said to himself: They are leaking word that it will be the east so I may assume that they will really come from the west. If I wait for them in the east, they will strike to the west.

My father would smile, hiding the embarrassment that my mother's words caused him, and she would go on with her story: But they really did come from the east, and they swept him away. So who was the cleverer one? I did not make this up! It is how he himself explained it to us, to make excuses for his defeat.

My father replied to my mother that Professor Kevork, her source of information and analysis, did not understand politics. So leave him to his little tunes, my father concluded. Little tunes? said my mother, on the point of tears. *Music*, my father corrected himself, conceding that much. Tell Professor Kevork that it is not a question of cleverness. Tell him that Jirjis Mitri says to him—after the usual greetings—that quite simply it is just like the position of the goalkeeper at the moment of a punitive strike—a penalty, tell him—just a minute before, a second before. East or west, to my right or to my left, the foot will kick the ball. What does cleverness or brain size have to do with any of this?

Now wait a minute! says my mother. War is not football. And then, of course it is a question of brains. When the goalkeeper stares into the eyes of the player before him, he must know . . . or he exercises some sort of psychological force over the player that influences the way his foot moves. That is cleverness, brains. Why do the Israelis always know what we are thinking?

Because they stare into our eyes, says my father, sarcastically but with bitterness this time. If they had looked into the eyes of Professor Kevork then we would have won the Six-Day War.

All you have is the feeble humor of the pathetic, says my mother, her voice trembling.

No, says my father. But once the goal came in among us, who knew what to do with the ball in our hands? You are right . . . I have the feeble humor of the pathetic.

Their number, I kept repeating to myself as I tied my bundle firmly around my middle. I have to be braver in any case, a little braver. I will not pee in my pants or nearly so every time the dogs' jaws come in sight.

Again I began to convince myself that it was necessary to reach a state of reasonable coexistence, without any bloody confrontations. Perhaps what I had done today, peeing along every step of my route so far, had been a good start. I thought again about returning home along the route I had sketched out in my mind, which would close the hypothetical circle, and pondered my experiment, which at the very least had not yet been established as a failure, since I could still maintain that whether or not they had sniffed my urine they had certainly not come right up to me.

I began to walk toward the Byblos, thinking about the penalty dilemma that, in my view, had not been solved. It had no solution. Both of them, my mother and my father, were right, but I gave preference to my father's opinion, on the grounds that it is very difficult to have a psychological influence over the player when he is at a distance from you. He is not looking into your eyes or hearing your words. He is looking at the goal cage or at the ball and hearing the roar of the crowds, their yells and the beating of his heart. Or am I simply finding—as usual—a way to stand by my father, and an excuse to find him in the right?

No . . . the penalty dilemma was a real dilemma, even if it had some points of similarity to war and Nasser's story.

Before I turned from the back of Cinema Byblos toward Souq al-Hisba I saw him crossing the street in front of me, without a glance in my direction. Two members of the pack followed him.

How could I not have noticed them circling around me? They had slunk in, then, from Rue Cadmus. I would not be able to get any further now toward home.

They were crossing the street, coming and going without turning in my direction, cutting off all routes toward my home and toward the sea. They crisscrossed the street, coming nearer and nearer to me each time. So. This was their plan for seizing me, hunting me down collectively in the open space of Place des Martyrs. He was following me, step by step, and his followers would block me from both sides so that they all could converge on me.

This time I was not frightened completely out of my wits. Perhaps it was because I was certain that I would die very soon. Or perhaps it was my need to move quickly, and I could not have fear paralyzing my movement.

I began to run straight up from Place des Martyrs until I reached Rue Bishara al-Khoury and dove into the entry of Théatre Shushu. The whole pack must be right behind me, I thought, but I heard no commotion or barking. I went out into the street. A few meters away I found him. His two sidekicks, I thought, must be close by. He held himself rigid, motionless, looking at me again but with a wide stare this time. Now he will attack, I said to myself. But he did nothing. The entryway to Théatre Shushu was no good as a refuge, obstructed as it was by mounds of rubble. I would have had to cross the street to get into the Samadi Center, whence I could disappear into the maze of buildings in the city center, and maybe from there I could make it as far as the Lazarists' College if he were the only one to follow me, without his two canine helpers. But he was much quicker than I was, and he would leap on top of me long before that.

But why hadn't he done so as I was running all this way, running to the spot where I stood now?

Why was he standing so still and stiff like that, giving me space, leaving me an opportunity to escape again? Why was he following me but not attacking me?

I started to stare at him, howling as loud as my throat could manage. He did not answer me. He did not move.

Then it came to me in a flash of understanding. He did not prey on the living. He was a dog who had returned to the wild, but he was not a wolf. He ate cadavers, and now he was sending me to my death. He was waiting for me to die so that he could eat me. He was only a bad dog; where would he have acquired the valiant nature of forest wolves?

So this is it, son of a bitch! I began to shout in the middle of the street. But when I saw his companions coming up behind him I shot off like the wind. Instead of going into the Samadi Center, though, I found myself heading toward Dabbas Square, going the length of Rue de la Mère Jilas. There I mounted the church steps, or rather the white stones that remained, caught my breath and looked around. I saw no trace of the dogs. That did not mean a thing, I told myself.

Now I must make a fast decision. Should I follow Rue Damas toward the bank of sandbags, or should I retrace my steps and disappear underground in the hole in Mar Jirjis Cathedral, cross as I had before, and then come out from the opening nearest to my house after resting to regain my forces and to give the dogs time to tire and forget?

I did not hesitate long. I heard the howling rise from many points, all of them nearby. It seemed to me as if darkness fell suddenly, like the time when I nearly drowned as a boy.

I began to walk down the Damascus road. I did not run or turn to look behind me. I walked as if out for a stroll. I remembered that I had not eaten for days, and suddenly I felt painfully hungry. And thirsty. I might die of hunger and thirst before anything else, I thought. Pliny the Wise— as my father called him—had died of apoplexy when he heard the explosion of a faraway volcano, just after he had been spared, by a simple and happy coincidence, from dying under the ruins of Pompeii. And the Father of Tragedy, Aeschylus the Great—as I call him, and as every one of God's creatures calls him too—died when his head was split open, because an eagle stalking a tortoise, who wanted to break its shell against a rock, confused the rock with the head of Aeschylus the Great, Father of Tragedy, who was bald. Very probably he had lost the hair on his head because of how intensely he had thought about the tragedy of humanity . . . and of human greatness too.

I threw my stick away. I took off my empty pack and walked in a straight line, not turning to look behind me. I knew that I was less than a stone's throw from the sandbags, and from the people behind them . . . in the land of the wars.

W hat do you do to me, Shamsa?

Why is it that from you I learn the grace of things, while from me you learn the absence of grace and the agony of attaining its fullness?

Is it because you are wiser than me, and more modest, more adept at making your incandescent self a reality? Is it because you are less fearful of the danger, and the threat, that loss poses?

What are you doing to me, Shamsa, when you torment me? You stay away, and then you return with blithe phrases that you are perfectly aware of having selected for their buoyancy, and because they will not have filled your absence for me or lessened the heaviness of it. There are the stories about your absence that you recount to me, unaware of their cruelty. You narrate them only that they may confirm the weight of this absence and its unshakeable place in my heart as you come to me; that you may erase all of my doubts through the legitimacy of the excuses that I have invented for you and that I have trained myself to believe until I have all but succeeded. You come to tell me that you have been elsewhere, not to tell me why you have not been here.

It is as if you want me to grow and mature through the successive days of my life—and to become more humble as well. You wish me to know that people are something less than their bodies, something less than their determination to hold themselves in the crescendo of pleasure toward the infinite. For when the crescendo exceeds the moment of its own meaning, nothing remains but the dissolution and corruption of notes unconnected. To leave the crescendo at its very summit is to deliver it from its own decay and from an ugly dissonance.

You stay away that you may return, in compassion for me. But I do not learn, I do not heed the admonitory lesson. I suffer in agony the more you recount to me, triflingly, heedless, the feeble reasons for your absence, to more perfectly enclose that void, to preserve it by the very moments of your proximity, a presence that does not brook apology. And I know that I have begun to lose this presence. I know that I lose more of it as time goes on, for I can see it now only as a thing surrounded, beseiged by your absence, a thing even redundant to it. I torture myself by savoring your presence; and as I witness my own suffering—painful, harmful, futile as it is—I can only suffer all the more. Each time you come to my home, each time you stay longer, the more pressing your absence from it becomes for me. I have disfigured the beauty of your presence for myself, as I try each time to fill the absence that it portends. It is as if, when you are with me, I empty the water that I have today in the baskets of yesterday, themselves now lost to me. In my stupidity. You open your arms and instead of finding the scent of cardamom I find the odor of sulfur. Instead of the fragrance of your neck I smell the scorching in my heart. As if I have become enamored of myself, not of you, and I don't know how to stop the wheel of my own loss.

When I try to speak, to offer excuses, Shamsa laughs. She says: It is the blessed wheel of time, not the wheel of your loss. Did I not teach you the mandragora?

I learned all that you taught me, Shamsa, and from my knowledge I drew benefit: sage augments perspiration, and the castor-oil plant assuages catarrh. The flower of galanga maintains healthy gums, and chamomile aids sleepless eyelids . . . . No, protests Shamsa. I remind you now of mandragora, because knowledge does not reside only in things that easily show their plain utility, but also in what lies locked within the secret of this usefulness. Do you remember the mandragora plant with its strengthening properties? How it takes flight inside the earth, how it disappears and stops growing and, deep underground, assumes the female or the male sex? How it tells its secret to whomever it chooses, and kills the ignorant one who uproots it unthinkingly? How it oscillates between poison and elixir, between death and tempestuous pleasure, between manifest presence and concealed absence?

It is up to you to choose . . . or you can rest content with chamomile and its many and undoubted benefits. You can choose whatever woman you want, whatever pleasure . . . you can also hesitate as much as you want and so lose, for you know that the mandragora descends into the earth and disappears completely or takes forms that it is often very difficult to recognize. Perhaps for the one who desires it, that is better than transformation into fatal poison.

My agony prevents me from learning, from bowing to the admonition, Shamsa. Only those possessed of cool heads and wisdom can comprehend the mandragora and its secret. Yet my head catches fire whenever I stand behind the windowpane, bewildered: what might be keeping you from appearing to me at the head of the street? The lesson is never learned by the one who stands teetering on the razor's edge of your absence, the threat ever-present that he will tumble into the void on one side that marks your continuing absence, or into the depths on the other side, the depths of your presence, which only tunnels deeper to settle your absence there, to confirm an absence that can offer no hope of return.

I learned no cautionary lesson from the mandragora, but you did learn lace. Perhaps because I knew toward what lesson we were proceeding together, my rogue knowledge led me . . . perhaps because you were innocent of my knowledge, you were able to learn, freed as you were of any fearful awe of the lesson to come . . . .

I was aware that our course had shifted, toward the curse of silk . . . . And so, when Shamsa stopped to ask me about samite, I gave away nothing. Afraid, I responded in a way that could only return her to lace's path.

Why do you wonder about the weaving of samite? In the disposition of its threads this fabric is a type of raw silk; but the color, or the numerous colors, are part of the design of the weave itself: the cloth's hues and shadows change as the cloth moves or trembles. True Damascene silk, that which came from Damascus and which we taught to the Persians and exported to the whole world, was an initial exercise in lace-making, for it offered a means of expressing light and shade, negative and positive. But it remained a game that one's eyes could play, a source of uncomplicated joy for the psyche, since it was not elevated above that single planar surface, there to mix with the air, to open imagination's appetite to a lust for the suggestive and the allure of a brush with vice, in stripping naked what is kept cloaked and veiled.

To attain lace in its truest form, Venice had to exist. For Venice composed the perfect blend of those essential elements, earth and water, to yield the sort of exceptional beauty that arises from those coincidences whose provenance we cannot fathom no matter how hard we try. Water mingling with dry earth, light with reflections of light; a thing akin only to miracles or sin, and so caught in an ineluctable flight from time. Venice had to exist for lace to become the ultimate luxury that threads could offer, in the game they played of concealment and revelation; in the filament's mercurial temper and its coy elusiveness even as the eye catches it. It could happen only in a state that knew a measure of wealth and luxury such that the allure of iniquity's touch would bespeak a permissible—indeed, a supererogatory—act.

It had to happen: the aristocrats of Spina, Aquila, Adria, Altinum, and Padua had to flee the raids of the barbarians for a place those hooves and lances could not gain, where the skilled architects could devote themselves to constructing their dreams in a space of no more than seven kilometers square. The heart of this new and unparalleled city emerged to surpass imaginations and dreams, so dazzling that it led the designers astray as they assigned numbers to streets and buildings. When they renumbered, writing the numbers in red over the earlier black, they erred again, and so left it to the humors of the water whether to open or close the streets to pedestrians, establishing in its ebb and flow its own numbering and its particular geometry.

The more precise the architecture of lace and the more regular and calculated its disposition of stitches to the eye, the more imagination works to destroy it and the more desire determinedly forgets the utility of figures. Calculating the stitches of lace is only as strict as its ruin requires, only severe enough to guarantee the eye's destruction in its perusal. Only the net that is designed with precision will attract the falling fish. Only the trap crafted perfectly and with consummate skill can kill.

"Punto in aria," said the people of Venice. "A point, or stitch, of air." They introduced lacework into the heavy density of brocade and velvet to elevate those fabrics to the complexity of inimitable contradiction. But for this they elected the edges of garments, where the cloth lightly strokes the points of desire. Exactly in the places where the skin shimmers through, and where the heartbeat pulses . . . exactly in the places where we deposit drops of perfume: the nape of the neck, the rises of the hollows across the shoulders, the throat and its plunging slope that glides between the breasts just where they begin to quiver and glisten, the wrists, and the line along which the kiss moves toward the interior of the palm, turned skyward for the lips to touch. There, lace entered. There, vision blended into legend, skin into desire, the eyelid into the moisture of the lips.

Shamsa laughed as she looked at me from within the perforations of the black lace that shrouded her to her hips. Why, she asked me, why were they so late in seeing what had been directly before them since the start of creation? Shamsa slipped her hand across her lower belly. Why, she asked me, why, then, did God make this frothy down for us, and put it precisely here, exactly where the slip toward the end of desire—as you call it—occurs? Is not this the beginning of lace, so that one can see what is not to be seen, and so that one does not see? Why were they so slow to see?

Perhaps they did not dare, Shamsa, I told her. Perhaps they did not dare. Perhaps they did not possess the necessary human presumption, the vital pomp and wealth, the city-state whose beauty exceeded the dreams of the architects and rose on the decision of its creators above the face of the water, in a challenge that was almost blasphemous, nearly heretical.

Lace was luxury upon luxury, exemplifying the wisdom that to the

one who has will be given, and multiplied. As if the oceans of the world were but canals to transport the gold and silver of the globe to Venice as the price of acquiring the point of air. Lords sold their castles and lands, their serfs, and their mills for the sake of a length of lace crafted with six million four hundred thousand throws of a shuttle. Provinces went to ruin, principalities collapsed, and thrones shook, among them the great throne of France. But then that sly fox Colbert decided to stanch the flow. Who, I wonder, could possibly have been able to understand the danger posed by the labyrinths of thread better than this son of a cloth merchant, Jean-Baptiste Colbert?

Colbert did not let the grass grow under his feet. For he knew that the wily Louvois and all the false nobility were lying in wait for him. He knew also that the humor of the Sun King would not be tempered for long by the balance-sheets of state coffers and public finances, and that he would be curbed only temporarily by the counsels of a minister who was, despite the praises of Mazarin, merely the son of a cloth merchant.

Colbert amassed his own weight in gold and silver, chose the most beautiful courtesans, and traveled in secret to Venice. Under the cover of night he met the head of the private ateliers of the grand Doge. He gave the man all he demanded without any negotiation or evasion. The man made the sign of the cross and hastily asked forgiveness of Saint Mark, his legs plunged into the darkened waters of the square. Between the sleeping palace of the Doge and the clock tower on which stood the Two Moors, the light of the moon shone but faintly on the domes of the Basilica, such that its grandeur did not inspire in him any terror, or humility, or remorse.

From the deck of his boat Colbert smiled broadly as he gazed at the golden sphere atop the Customs Building. Now, he murmured to himself, the stitch made of air had become his, and he would carry it to Alençon before the sun had reached its zenith. Now the supports beneath the golden dome of Customs at the entry to the port of Venice must swallow a modicum of the city's pride.

But the lucky Colbert, smiling in the shadow of the deck of his sloop as it carried him away from the port of Venice, did not know that the covetous, intriguing Catherine de Medici, and all of those women after her who would slip into the beds of the kings of France, and even the greedy Marie Antoinette, would send the price of a simple bobbin of lace thread above one hundred forty pieces of gold. They fired the appetites of the monopolists who fixed the wages of the poor lace-makers, to the point of pushing those women to take off their own *culottes*, to join the revolutionaries, to leap into the fire of revolution fever that ran in the streets like volcanic red lava . . . . The poor women of Bruges, on the other hand, were able to go on living from their needles and hooks, far from the destruction of the revolutions, because they were convinced that the Virgin Mary herself had taught the virgin maidens to weave lace in order to sustain themselves, and because the monopolists of Bruges, and of all of Belgium at that time, did not comport themselves on the same level of greed as the French and their women. Most significant of all, Bruges, its buildings and streets over the water, was—and still is—called Little

Venice, because it so resembled the republic of St. Mark, protected by its two so very courageous lions.

What do you do to me, Shamsa?

I had not become acquainted with the misery that wisdom brings. No one told me, no one taught me that what one gives, one loses. Loses, and pays dearly.

Perhaps it was because I gave you what was not mine to give. Perhaps it was because I taught you without having the learned skill of a teacher. For you, I dipped from the sack of another, all the while filled with the arrogance of doers of good, almsgivers, and the openhanded. I fell a victim to my own poor, scanty knowledge. The lessons of my upbringing deceived me; or I did not understand those lessons as I should have.

I believed those who told me that the more we give, the more our wealth increases; the more room we make for others, the roomier becomes the house; the more we dip, the fuller become our pots and our bags.

No one told me that I should count my possessions. No one counseled modesty, so that I would recognize the boundaries of my domain. No one drew my hand away from the dipper, or held me back from the pot or the sack, before I could offer the bulk of its sparse content.

Or, I wonder, did I not understand the lesson as I should have, my pride delivering me into meet retribution, your absence. Your loss, a dark well whose smooth walls I could not cling to unless I could summon hatred of you, could accuse you of betrayal, of deception, of theft, of a stab in the back . . . and then you would return.

Did I myself learn what I taught you? Did I understand it? Or, I ask myself, did I fall under the spell of my own speech, so intoxicated that I could not grasp what you saw in the yonder of my words, behind the cloudiness of my assertions that so demanded your pity? My body's soreness afflicts me, now; all the parts of my body ache in the agony of my desire for you. The parts of my body, illuminated before my own eyes and in spite of myself, incandescent with their desire for you . . . the parts of my body afflict me now. Illuminated before my own eyes, in my incapacity and fatigue, impervious to any assertion of will and in spite of anything I might try to do.

The parts of my body glow in the anguish of my desire for you, like these fireflies that keep me company at night, illuminating my deep blackness since the oil lamp has gone out, a consequence of my lengthy absence from home.

When we were little we called them flying lamps of the night. We did not know that their phosphorescent light—so pretty, so blue—is nothing but a sexual organ flaming with desire for the female. We did not know that the glow is its moan of complaint against the loneliness of flying with only two wings, a call for rescue from the consuming flame of desires nested in the pain of the body's organs.

Sitting on my bench of stone, I lean slightly to follow the flight of the night's fireflies to the carob tree, now directly across from me. All I can detect of its shape is the impress of the lacy holes in its high branches upon the lilac sky.

Little by little, the number of fireflies grows and their staccato glow outlines the shape of the carob tree, now heavy with the chaotic cries of the males. From where I sit I see them erupt with the electricity of lust, fibrils let loose to play, charges that flicker and surge with crazed insistence.

Then, little by little, the flicker grows more regular, acquires a rhythm, pulses with stern order. The tiny lights assemble themselves into a single secret code flaring and fading in harmony, their rhythm unspoiled by any flawed movement or stray motion.

What could have contrived the key to that code but the superior intelligence of instinct? It is as if the fireflies know that when scattered they will meet only failure and find their members burned; as if they know that their luck in attracting females lies in their arboreal orchestra in the fullness of its tempo . . . a completeness that inheres in the tree and its nighttime becoming a single male, a single desire . . . high, ear-piercing, and ordered.

And me . . . I am one, alone; I flare and then fade uselessly, in a night that refuses to burn steadily with me and leaves me in my flawed, idled instinct to my own chaos, to my loneliness and insignificance. Behind the window, I hold to my own tree. You come to me; you do not come to me; you come to me; you do not come; you do, you do not . . . to my own tree, alone.

I began to pat Thalj's neck, as he lay near my feet . . . How are you faring, Thalj? Do you need only to let go with a loud howl for your woman to appear? Teach me, Thalj.

I named him Thalj—for the snow that we get so thickly in the mountains sometimes—because his fur was so white, but even more because when I opened my eyes to the lapping of his tongue on my face, the light of day dazzled me, and it appeared to me, from my sleep that must have been long and deep, that snow covered everything around me with a brilliantly glistening, delicate layer.

I had realized that they had missed me, and that I was still very much alive, when I saw the corpses around me all swollen, and smelled the odor of putrefaction. I knew also, from the shards of images flickering through my head, that I had awoken several times with the weight of those who had died pressing down on me, and had pushed them off; and that I had heard gurgling sounds issuing from open throats and fast growing quiet, extinguished as the throats filled with rain water that pelted down hard, so violently that it deafened my ears and returned me to my sleep.

At that moment I felt no fear of the dog who licked my face from above, even though it had been that same dog who, earlier, had pushed me on further, whether he and his sidekicks meant to do so or not, until they seized me at the armed barrier at the outer limit of the sandbags. I sensed immediately that he did not intend to make me his prey. Then I remembered that as I fled from him and before I reached the barrier, I had doubted seriously that he was even capable of stalking living things.

I stood up to look around and to study the dog. I reminded myself that I had gone of my own accord to the armed barrier, and it was my own stupidity that had pushed me, as usual.

Bemused, I began to walk. The dog followed me closely and I was soon persuaded that from the beginning all he had wanted was my company. He did not mean me any harm or enmity. He wanted a human being as a friend and master; he longed for a sociability that would resemble whatever had disappeared, one day, behind the roadblocks. Perhaps it was a longing for that owner who had abandoned him on one particular day, or had died and left him grudgingly. In me he found a creature who reminded him of the one who had gone off without saying goodbye.

I walked all the way down to Place des Martyrs as he tracked me, staying close behind. I no longer felt afraid of anything—now, after the spraying bullets had missed me, when they forced us to stand in a single line against the wall. They threw our bodies over on the other side of the sandbags, believing that we had all died, or were about to die, as blood spurted from the holes that the bullets had left in us. I must have fallen to the ground out of sheer terror before the bullets could reach me, and then the bodies of others must have covered me, or at least the body of whoever was nearest to me on my left. That was the direction from which the spraying had begun, at the hands of the man charged with the task of 'dispatching' us, as his superior said to him, following a conversation on his walkie-talkie with those in charge.

I thought about returning there to bury all of the corpses, but I dismissed that idea rather quickly when I recalled the stench. Every child of Adam meets the fate his Lord designs for him, I told myself. And perhaps dogs were part of this fate.

I sat in front of the Café Laronda, at Zayn the juice vendor, catching my breath. I saw the dogs scampering to and fro in front of Azar Coffee Roastery. They did not come near us. Then the ears of the dog beside me stood straight up, his body shook and he stiffened in place, looking toward his companions. As he was running toward them, and then disappearing with them in the streets of the little souqs behind Azar Coffee Roastery, I named him Thalj. I smiled, admiring the whiteness of his fur and guessing that his white color rather than his strength was behind his leadership of the pack that he seemed to leave and rejoin at his fancy, just like leaders of people, while the rest remained a group that rarely broke up into individuals.

I strolled to the small pond encircled by cane near the Parliament Building. Despite the coolness of the air, the strong rays of sun sent a delicious heat into me once I had taken off my dirty rags. I picked a large bouquet of 'glass grass' and lowered myself into the water to bathe, savoring the thick foam and the fragrance of the water. I felt sorry for myself and a little sad when I saw how skinny my arms were above the water. They appeared extraordinarily long, stretching further away from my body than seemed quite right.

Coming out of the water, I sat down on a clean stone and extracted the remaining filth and dirt from beneath my long nails. I felt hunger pressing on my intestines, as I used to feel as a little boy after coming out of the bath. But I stayed where I was, waiting until I was completely dry, running my fingers through my hair so it would dry quickly and the warmth would return to every part of my body. I felt something and realized that lice had colonized my scalp. Disgusted, I asked myself how I could go home and sleep on my fabrics in this state. I pulled up some nettles, being careful not to prick myself, braided them and thrust them into my hair, hopeful that they would rid me swiftly of the lice. I examined my armpits and pubic hair: everything was clean and free of infestation, blackness glistening against the whiteness of my skin. Good.

Naked and light, I walked down the slope toward the Omary Mosque.

Before reaching Rue Weygand I found what I had hoped to find. The little date palm was still there, and the fruit still hung upon it, now ripe. I shimmied up the trunk easily, began to pluck the sweet dates, and ate until I was full. Carrying some fronds thick with fruit, I turned, happy and serene, toward home, asking myself what state I would find the garden and verandah in, without feeling at all anxious about the answer.

My father was not a mere cloth trader, as my mother so likes to say. Don't believe her, and don't listen too hard or too long to her fabrications, I said to Shamsa, who knocked on my door one evening after I had grown weary of my long bouts of standing at the window, waiting for her to appear at the head of the street.

Why did you come this evening, Shamsa? Why do you come when I am not here and what do you want from my elderly, babbling mother and her lying, embroidered sentences? Don't you trust me? Don't you believe the narratives that I have for you?

Yes, says Shamsa, but you do not tell me the whole story. Why are you not teaching me silk?

Because the right time has not come.

You said that silk has many stories. Teach me the first one, and then I will wait.

I will, very soon.

You are lying to me. You have not yet brought any silk to me here. You promise me the story, and then you don't tell it. To draw me back, you promise me, and I come back, wanting to hear an end that does not come, a story that does not even begin.

As Shamsa spoke she stood opposite me, as if to threaten me with her exit and then her departure—with the absence that would bind me like a foaming dog to the windowpane.

I dropped to the floor and sat cross-legged on the carpet, trying to keep hidden my fierce longing to burst into loud sobs. I smiled instead, and cleared my throat as I do when I start our stories. She did not succumb to temptation; she remained standing. I gazed at her, fondly but reproachfully, and she smiled. I put out my hand to the hollow at her Achilles' tendon just above the ankle, and enclosed it in my palms. She did not move back. I moved nearer, put my arms around her leg, and rested my head against the top of her thigh. I began to stroke the back of her leg, all the way to the hollow at the knee where there are the two dimples that inflame my fancy when she is away from me and I remember that tensed sinew that pulses quickly in one of them. I raised my hands to her hips, pressing them gently so that she would turn, and she did. My lips to the hollow carved out by the dimples, I moved with my quick, feverish kisses from the backs of her knees to her thighs, in terror at the possibility that she would slip away from me.

First I felt her fingers planted in my hair, and then she clutched at it, turned to me, and dropped down onto her knees. As she looked into my eyes with her lids half closed I told myself that if she were to kiss me on the mouth I would have gained half the distance, and then I would not lose hope. If she kisses me on the mouth, I thought to myself, it means that she has less power over me than I tend to think she has, when I am suffering from her remoteness.

I did not bring my face any nearer to hers. I told myself that I would leave no space for an ambiguity that, later on, could rekindle my doubt. I will not shorten that distance, I will not go halfway to her mouth. I must restrain myself firmly, with the fiber of certainty that binds me now to her half-closed eyes, to the parted lips on which a reddish saliva shines. I must tauten the fiber of my strength now, just a little; for if it breaks, it will at once shred the tension in desire's tendon, leaving my body crumpled like rags in a heap, in agony and utter impotence. And regret.

I did not bring my face nearer to hers. My mouth dry and my breath quickening, I resisted my body's slide into a state of numbness. If I let go of my alert resistance, my desire will devour me, the ferocity of my yearning will consume me. And so will my regret.

If she does not bring her lips nearer and kiss me on the mouth I will hold onto my last card. I will not make love to her. If she does not bring her lips closer and kiss me on the mouth, and yet I sleep with her, she will go away never to return. If I am able, if I have the strength to sleep with her despite my certainty, despite seeing myself facing that final loss that I will not be strong enough to endure, she will not return.

Her mouth. Her mouth. Her mouth . . . no movement of my head. I work my brain to reckon the distance so that I will not bring my head forward unawares, so that it will not move of its own accord, without my willing it. So that my upper spine will not betray me.

I do not close my eyes lest she take that as an invitation to bring her mouth closer. Now I am playing my last card, my eyes open, my gaze steady. I look into her eyes not at her mouth. I keep my head steady, rigid against its hidden convulsion, when it looks to me like the distance is growing shorter and that she is coming closer with her red mouth that I cannot see. A scorching film coats my wide-open eyes but I do not blink. Blackness sweeps across my wide-open eyes and I know that her mouth is on mine.

I close my eyes. I close my eyes over tears that she will not see, not right now. I let my blood collect in my mouth until I can almost taste its warmth. I am not anxious about the abrupt withdrawal of my blood from my member, emptying it completely, because I know how the circulation must proceed now that it has begun as I wanted it to begin; as it must begin. I am not anxious about the strength draining from my body, because the flaming wave will return now, with such force that it will all but split the skin cells as it collides against the barricade of her, before its steam evaporates, shiny as the sweat across her face that moistens mine with its salt. The taste of her lips has turned fleshy and their raw flavor I cannot eat. I draw back from her lips and my tongue licks them as I try to dampen my very real desire to eat them. I draw away from her neck. I bite her shoulder lightly and push her body away from me to better see it. To see that I can after all separate from her, to see that I am not drowning in her flesh. She pulls off whatever clothes she still had on and lies down on her back; with a quick movement she has flicked off the light in the corner, and it dawns on me that we are now at the other end of the sitting room and that night has fallen, darkening every corner of the house.

Shamsa comes back from the bathroom, her long red hair dripping. I see that she has wrapped herself in a big towel and has not put her clothes back on, and so I ask her if she will stay here tonight. That depends on the story, she says. If listening to it tempts me, I will stay. If what I learn entices me . . . .

Tonight I will tell you the story that will lead us to silk. And so that we may enter that final chapter, we must arm ourselves with special learning, with a broad knowledge that makes us more cannily receptive to it, raising us to the story's level so that we will not fall victims of its magic. For knowledge is dangerous to the uninformed who are unprepared to receive it. It is not simply a matter of knowledge passing them by, or of losing its pleasure . . . for, as you taught me about the mandragora, from being an elixir it can become a deadly poison.

And my father, who taught me all of this and gave me the long training of a true disciple, was not a mere trader in cloth. He was a man of knowledge; he had penetrated the secret. And thus he waited the right amount of time, waited until I had matured and could see the woman in my mother and the man in him; and so when our number was counted we would be three, no fewer; and so when our succession was reckoned, from my emigrant grandfather to myself, we would be three generations and no fewer.

He would have preferred to reserve a longer period of learning for me, my father told me, to let my knowledge ripen so that I could advance with him in the story, side by side; so that it would reveal itself to us together rather than my learning it from him. But the era of decadence—the age of Diolen, as he called it—beleaguered us, and his illness and premonition of imminent death assailed us. And so here I am, courting the peril of telling all of this to you, when you are still ripening; but you, too, besiege me with your insistence and your haste, and you take up forbidden weapons when you threaten to stay away. So listen well, because we are together—you and I—setting sail toward the same adventure.

Let us begin at the beginning—as my father would say—at the point from which our migrations commenced, to spread the world over. They began on the shores of west Africa, where the wise people of the Dogon say that in the beginning the Lord—the Word of Creation—was a breath that brought into being the fibrous plants and the animals that produce the fur and down in which we covered our skins of old. But the word 'Lord'—composed of connected letters and requiring the whole mouth to utter—goes back to the fourth djinni, Ogo, who rebelled against the Lord with the aid of the spider in the tree, who lured and tempted him. If that cunning spider was evil, the tree was a blessed and devout one. It flourished and spread its branches toward the four corners of the universe, only to return and wrap itself tightly around the spider. The tree arrested the spider's arrogant reach and the harm it could do, and then the tree suffocated the spider so that it could not carry out its rebellion, which was to weave a web across the surface of the earth. Humanity retrieved the word 'Lord' only after a long period of disbelief that lasted until the birth of the seventh djinni, ancestor of the new human, whom the Lord created in the form of a loom. Thus would he carry the words of the Lord to humanity, embodied in eighty threads of cotton, forty above for the warp, plied, and forty lower ones for the weft, single strands laid out like the teeth in a mouth. The warp and the weft moved up and down like the rhythm of the jaws, while the bobbin of thread formed the throat and the shuttle was the tongue.

In the language of the Dogon, the word *sawah* meant 'fabric' and also 'speech,' and at the same time it signified the embodied deed . . . a naked woman, for example, was called a 'mute' woman. In Arabic, look at the consonance of letters in *haki*, the telling of a tale, and *hiyaka*, weaving!

The weaver is the one who 'makes' speech, and a person 'wears' his words. And after the weaver listens to his grandfather, the third *nomo,* who breathes from his pharynx the sacred word and pulls and ties the threads of life together, he transmits these to other men by his weaving and the secret calculations that underlie it . . . but like the priest, he gives or bequeaths the secret of weaving only to those who have gained the necessary knowledge, the gnosis; to those who deserve it in their aptitude and their wisdom, and with the blessing of the ancestors.

Planting and tilling the soil are but the weaving of life, the coming and the going, like the movements of a loom, and like the cycle of day and night coming to us in rotation, and like the linkage between sky and earth, life and death. Even the bold traveler–adventurer Marco Polo employed the act of tilling to describe the techniques of Persian silk weaving . . . .

And as it is with us—we Christians, Shamsa—for the Dogon, people are born sinful. But they are purified of original sin, of transgressing that first prohibition, through weaving. They must weave by the dictates of the sacred tradition, and must pass through each degree of sacred knowledge . . . they bury shuttle and bobbin with the deceased, after wrapping the body in a shroud, square-shaped in black and white, woven with a single strand that is never cut and therefore never blemished by a knot. For to cut the yarn means loss, precisely as it will mean for Ariadne, daughter of Minos and sister of Phaedra, whose strand saved her from dying in the labyrinth. To break or cut that thread, dyed along alternating lengths, white and black, is to break the relationship of day to night, to fall into the void, into nonexistence and oblivion.

And because we forget, Shamsa, and because in our ignorance we deny truths, we have forgotten that the weaver, wherever he may be on this earth, is trustee of the secret of life and peace, a secret forever menaced by the victory of death and war. Is not nakedness—the loss of clothing—linked indissolubly to original sin, to retribution, and to a ceaseless striving for atonement? Look at the figure of the Goddess Athena: in one hand she holds a spindle and in the other a spear, in one hand the wisdom of creating cloth and in the other the woes and destruction of wars. Think of the sage Gandhi, who took up weaving as he faced the English because according to the Indian myth, the goddess demanded that the warrior caste transform themselves from fighters into weavers. If they did so, then she could grant them an existence that would remain eternally free in the grace of each day's dawning, a renewal emerging from the darkness of night.

If the weaver entrusted with the secret is a man, the goddess who teaches and inspires is always a woman, my dear Shamsa. A woman who casts light from darkness, white from black. Those goddesses—Athena, Persephone, Ishtar the Babylonian—were called moon mistresses, for from the glow of the moon they spun the light of the coming day. And when they had no more to spin the world would reach its end, to plunge forever into eternal darkness. The Sumerian goddess of weaving, Tagtog, taught us that every pass of the shuttle on the loom weaves the words of our ancient ancestors, the words that enrich the memory we inherit and that we enrich in our turn. And when the words of the grandfathers begin to be forgotten, the knots and threads in the weaving begin to come undone and the world ends in fragments, shapeless, a dust cloud in the nebula.

Just as you are listening to me, lovely Shamsa, we listen to the words that come to us from the distant sky, wherever we may be. In China the weaver of the world, dispatcher of the heavens' words, is the thousandth star in the constellation of the Lyre. Both the loom and the art it creates, she spins through the year and weaves at her loom on the banks of the Milky Way. Within another constellation lies the plow, symbol of the earth's weaving as it comes and goes through the soil, pulled by the Great Bear's chariot. The spring equinox is the meeting of the weaver with the plow, the balance of the two principles of the world, the yin and the yang.

Do you see now how all of the stories resemble each other, how they come together, whatever their origins? The Phoenicians, too, believed that the Lord wove earth and sky with the filaments of His boundless wisdom, wrapping a cosmic tree whose branches reached further and fuller than we can know. It is that Tree of Life that the East glorified— from Byzantium to Sassanid Persia to India—and that entered the West. At our death we fall from it like fruit that has ripened to fullness, to return to the cycle of existence through its celestial fields and the infinity of its branches. And the daughters of Zeus, the Greeks' god of gods, are three: the eldest is the spinner who pulls the thread of our days from the light of the sky. The second is the weaver, who fills in the details of our lives and weaves our human fates. The third cuts the thread, ending our final breath. The peoples of the Mediterranean believed that clouds are lengths of cloth, unravelling to their first strands when the sky pours rain and there falls onto the earth blessed water.

Have you gotten sleepy, Shamsa?

Yes, a little, but my drowsiness is not a longing to sleep. It is rather how I open myself to the pleasures of words, how I follow the story. The parts of my body relax, so that I can forget them and so that I can train the alertness of my ears, my imagination, my understanding, onto the thread of your long and lovely tale. On your lips, the story revives your father's face and summons the wisdom of my Naqshbandi grandfather, lover of the firmaments, companion to the shepherds, weaver of linen and of goat hair, from which he crafted tents—that man walking the thread of his Lord's mercy to the rays of the ecstasy of the absolute, cloaked in the certitude of what the Lord of the Two Worlds has woven for him as the true Word.

Shall I go on then, and you will stay here tonight?

Until dawn, until the first thread on the spool of daylight appears . . . or when the blackness of the thread turns to white.

Good, Shamsa.

My father—who was not a mere trader in cloth—would have said that spinning, weaving, and sewing are not simply metaphors that help us to see how creation is reflected, to understand its past and how it came to be; they are not helpful only, as Plato said, in understanding that the world pivots on a sort of spindle of diamonds, in whose firmament spin planets and stars each according to its orbit and the rhythm of its rotation. No, it is more, for the politician is the artisan who crafts the social fabric. And as Plato said, so said Virgil when he named the god of the city on the island of Delos 'the Weaver.'

The techniques that go into clothmaking are in essence like the planning and construction of a city. It began when human beings plaited tree branches to mark out the space of their dominion against the surrounding land, and then wove those branches as a roof for the home, and also fashioned baskets in which to preserve the fruits of the earth as the garment preserves the fruits of the body before it preserves the body in its entirety . . . and later the maker of traps erected woven structures to enclose animals he had subdued and domesticated, bringing them into the sphere of his authority. Thus the domicile was born and multiplied, as in the story of Elissa of Tyre, weaving her thin strips of hide to mark the vast boundaries of Carthage. The home grew by accumulation, its outer margins expanding like the thread that spirals around the spindle's heart, circle upon circle. Around the column, the columnar memory of the grandfather, expand the rings made by the homes of children and grandchildren, always held within the magnetic field of kinship and inheritance. Colors take on emblematic meanings as they signify according to tribal divisions and birth hierarchies. Do not the colors of the tents on the heights of Aurès spell out the identity of each tribal group and trace its possession of surrounding territory? Does not the shaykh of the tribe—to this day—bless the raising of a new dwelling by saying: Woven fabric, you have been hoisted to become a home, in the protective shade of the Prophet Muhammad's mercy, God's prayers and peace be upon him. So protect, and be blessed . . . . And was not the home of the Jews—who walked for forty days in the dangerous desert behind their prophet Moses—the ark of the covenant that held ten carpets of linen? And do not the prayer rugs of all the Muslim faithful extend toward the mosque's *qibla,* and thence toward Mecca, to signify the architecture of their prayers' orientation, in the noblest direction, toward the House of God? Did not the Arabs designate their chief by knotting a thread in his direction? And, following from that, in the politics of groups and the administration of the city is it not the 'thread of authority' that designates leadership, 'knotted' only for those who comprehend the weave of the social, the secret of its stitches and knots, its fabric? There are two sorts of people who can destroy this careful work: those who come from outside the city walls, strangers with the vigor of youth who bear parchments on which are drawn new maps, scrolls held open through the desire to infiltrate and hybridize and form new connections; or ignorant leaders who draw the strength of their immediate authority from the weakness of the threads and the fatigue of the weave. Such are the enemies of their own cities and people, for they bring upon those folk destruction and death.

Ignorant also are those who do not know the magic of the thread and the curses that the fabric may bring. In their imperfect knowledge and the illusion of their self-importance, they are the ones who do not see that the work of the weaver has its dangers and its evil, dark reverses. Open your ears, Shamsa, and listen to what I have to say.

For when the thread begins to snarl and tangle, it becomes the net; it is entanglement. It is the trap, the deception, and the treachery; it is temptation, the enticement wrought by false suggestion. It is the descent into killing, the fall into the void.

The knotting of the strand that begins every piece of weaving unites two ends that will become a single yarn. One end lies in the hand of goodness and the other in the hand of evil; one end extends to the umbilical cord and the other to the hangman's noose. And just as we knot a strip of cloth and place it over an ailing part of the body, hopeful that the whole body will return to its pure and healthy state—to the moment when the umbilical cord was knotted at birth—and the illness will disappear, so we make knots in evil writing and black magic, in the thread of fates, to bring on illness and misery, madness and death. Did not the prophet Ezekiel say: Thus said Yahweh: Woe, woe to the women who make garments, despite the variety of sizes and people, to force souls to fall into their traps? Ever since the Assyrians, have we not inscribed our envy and our agony on a thread from the gown of the beloved that we knot with our sinful prayers so that no other lover interferes, and so that on the evening of our departure the beloved, alone, shrivels and dies, in the terrible solitude that we have left behind?

Was not Arachne, defying Athena by spinning, transformed into a spider, into the ugliest of the Lord's creatures, to spin under the curse that she would never complete her spinning because she was prohibited from wearing what she spun?

And how could the naughty Medea have killed her pretty young rival, Crios, without her poisoned gown soaked in the juices and acids of her envy, unquenchable by death alone since all humanity meets death? It was the agony of a long and slow death that Medea's poisoned gown brought about. But even that was not the culmination, for the corpse was cut to pieces and scattered over the ground to undo the fabric's weave. Even better, boil and eat the fragments to suck in the strength of its original fibers.

For there is no knowledge, Shamsa, but that which stands firm on the pinnacle. There is no knowledge but that which can see the two opposite sides together, white with black, and simultaneously. Whoever does not disclose that killing offers a fierce pleasure has gulled us, has dug before our feet a devilish trap into which we will surely tumble, easy prey to the false image of the angels. Whoever has not taught us the pleasure of the kill has slain us in his compassion for us and in his scorn for the entirety of our being.

But is it not the case that to remain at the pinnacle, and to see the two sides together and simultaneously, is an exercise in impossibility? Might not the compassion, and even the scorn, be a trap by which we protect those whom we love?

And to stand at the pinnacle of cloth is to stand within silk. Within the eye of the needle. And so my grandfather said to my father: Do not marry that woman. And do not return to that city.

The thread of day's emergence illuminated Shamsa's face, asleep on my arm, when my mother awoke and, from her room, called out to me.

W hen I awoke, the vigorous tang of frying *ta'liya* assailed my nose—garlic and coriander *ta'liya*, not the onion-based version. The sort that makes one's mouth water and flings the door of appetite wide open.

I went up onto the verandah, puzzling over why I felt such constant hunger these days. I hardly ever stopped eating; I seemed to spend the bulk of my day either searching for something to eat or treating myself for indigestion and pain in my digestive organs. I had not learned my lesson from the constipation that overwhelmed me, inflating my belly like a drum, after I came upon the fruit of half a field of Indian figs in front of the Restaurant Ajami. On top of that I consumed several dozen little cobs of maize, their sweet kernels tasting deliciously milky. If it had not been for the apricot tree in the Souq Bazarkan and the wild blackberry bushes at the Municipal Building whose fruits had grown to the size of the mulberries at the Mosque of Amin, the constipation would have poisoned my blood and finished me off.

This ravenous, greedy hunger comes to me like a rushing wave, irresistible like the sexual desire that sweeps through my body, seizing all of me instantaneously as if it has suddenly welled up from the ground in obedience to its own special gravitational pull. It slips into me escaping from the chaotic gusts of wind that sometimes come to me saturated with the odor of women, reeking with female smells no matter where I turn my nose. It is that sharp, particular fragrance that women carry, and it makes my head reel.

At these moments, usually, I stand at the edge of the verandah. I put my fingers in my mouth and whistle loudly and repeatedly to Thalj until he comes to me. After a few words that I presume he understands perfectly, we start running together. I run with all the force my knees can exert and my heart can stand, in whatever direction Thalj leads me, for he runs ahead and comes circling back to me hundreds of times. He urges me to run faster and jump higher. Sometimes, as we glisten with the oils our bodies make, the sweat breaking out over his fur and my skin, I have the feeling that he is pulling me. It is as if he binds me to his own body with a strong rope, as if he could almost fly with me, gliding many meters through the air. Like a pair of mad dogs, we run together, and in harmony we howl feverishly. It all boosts our enthusiasm, encouraging us to run on in spite of the pain in the limbs, the burning in the knees, and the whistling through the head. We dash ahead and leap over the rocks, over falling tree trunks, piles of destroyed walls, weedy hills, cavities made by tiny springs, piled-up warehouse security doors, stairs from lower floors . . . and at the end of the race we throw ourselves together into the big lake behind the Parliament, where we linger, held by the sweet water that we lap up. Our muscles cool down and a regular, quieter pulse returns.

But Thalj has noticed my flagging endurance on recent occasions; he can tell that I am not catching up to him as quickly as I used to do. And he has started to react to me with a showy aggression. One time, when I stopped running and sat down on a stone in front of the Bata Store to regain my breath, he started to growl, stalked toward me and bared his teeth, looking me in the eye and snarling at me. I did not hesitate. I stood up, walked slowly and steadily over to him, and with all the strength I could summon I slapped his skull. He sat down suddenly on his hind legs while I scolded and bellowed right over him. And when I returned to my stone, I watched him slink away toward Riad Solh Place, his tail held between his back legs.

Walking down Rue Maarad toward home, sweat pouring from every pore, I mused over the possible causes of my unanticipated weight gain. It was why all of this had happened, I told myself.

True, I am not a young man. But I have not become elderly in a matter of a few weeks. It is my voracious appetite and steady weight gain that are tiring me like this and slowing my movements—me, someone who has lived his entire life up until this moment either slender or downright scrawny.

Hajj Abu Abd al-Karim used to say to my father: Pay attention to your son! He is your only son. Don't you see how thin he is? Don't you know the reason for it, don't you remember yourself at his age? Take some interest in him, brother. It is not just a matter of food and nourishment, you know . . . he has other longings, which if they are unmet might make him sick or give him unhealthy thoughts. Aren't you aware that some young fellows of his age have gone mad for this reason?—you know as well as I do the one I have in mind. If you don't want to marry him off right now, help him to seek out other solutions. Help him to understand life, Hajj. From the goodness of your own understanding and knowledge, teach him. I can speak on your behalf to some folks who would take him to a place where he'd learn. There is no shame in it. This is God's will, and even a blessing from Him. Can you imagine how upset you would be if God had not put this blessing into him? Explain this to me, Hajj Abu Niqula, since you are a wise man. To whom do we give responsibility for our boys, to whose wisdom do we leave them when they are troubled? Who can take them by the hand before evil temptations devour them? Don't you see how pale he is?

And then Hajj Abu Abd al-Karim broke into a laugh, stymied by the blush that flamed on my father's face rather than on mine. He thought I could not understand his innuendos and it bewildered him to see my father so discomfited. I did not understand my father's chagrin either. I thought perhaps he was embarrassed by the spareness of his body next to the corpulence of Abu Abd al-Karim, whose face was always red, and likewise the stoutness of his son Abd al-Karim, who went regularly to the Fitness Center and lifted extremely heavy weights. I believed that my father was mortified to have such a thin son, so skeletal that the muscles seemed to knot inward rather than to bulge outward. I thought perhaps he envied the robust aura of Abd al-Karim, who with a mere slap or a single kick could crumple me into a heap on the floor, looking like nothing so much as an old rag. After my father had abandoned commerce and special imports to sit passively in the shop, not long before the war started, we often had to unload huge rolls of fabric from the trucks of the wholesale merchants. Even though I had matured fully by then, the handlers and shop assistants would rush to help me while Abd al-Karim hoisted an entire bolt by himself, despite his proud father's fierce scolding, audible as soon as he thought he had my father's attention. Raising his voice at his son, he abandoned temporarily the careful smile that would soon reappear, sketching itself discreetly across his lips once Abd al-Karim had swung his load off his shoulders and onto the floor.

Yes, I believed that my father's embarrassment stemmed from the suggestive phrases that Hajj Abu Abd al-Karim had tossed his way, or that it showed itself on my behalf, or that he was ashamed of his own thin frame that he had bequeathed to me. It was years before I understood his reaction. For I understood it only after I had listened furtively to the confessions of Professor Kevork, and then to my father's stifled sobs.

Now, though, I can hardly stop eating, as if whatever I swallow does not stay for any amount of time in my stomach and cannot fill it. I have experimented, chewing and swallowing things I never got close to before, plants or crawling things that cross the floor or birds that fall into my traps. Almost nothing repels me.

Scavenging?

In the little splinter of mirror that I found in the Cinema Metropole I can see only parts of my face and body. Therefore I cannot readily see my skin puffing out or my limbs filling up with fat. I see only the pudginess of my fingers and the way my breasts protrude, held up by my rotund belly when I sit down. I cannot even see my sex now, except when I try hard, when I'm pissing, or when my nose is assailed by female odors and I grow feverish with longing.

I can recall the plumpness of Shamsa's body, her pretty fullness before—before it began to dissolve. My fatness, though, I think of as ugly, and its bloated look must be a result of my gluttony—and of my age. It is deterioration. Decadence.

But how can it be so when I have not felt such lust since Shamsa left me? How can I have such a burning desire for food and for women if I am truly aging so? I no longer know how old I am, but certainly I have passed fifty. How can that be deterioration, when I have almost no control over my huge appetite, which opens itself to every sort of fulfillment?

These are the marks of deterioration, my father said as he helped me to move the heavy bolts of precious silks of all kinds to the room below ground. It is the disgraceful flaw of not being able to exert mastery over an appetite as cavernous as the mouth of an immense well, an inability to prefer, to select, to sort, to classify according to suitability and quality. It is the indiscriminate appetite of the cancerous cell in its voracious blindness. Sin and innocence simultaneously, inseparably—for how can you blame a blind person, who cannot see and so launches himself toward everything randomly? And because he cannot see a form, he cannot remember it.

Look around you a little. Look around, and then tell me what it is that we are selling now, that we display and offer for sale. Is it cloth, or is it cloth's chemical forgery? Where is the yarn in this weave, whose identity and origin we do not know? Tell me, does the customer name the cloth she wants or does she merely point to a color or motif? And when she touches it or manipulates it between her fingers, does she ask herself anything beyond whether it will make the vexing demand that she press it?

Who, these days, sees in a length of cloth its origin, its place of birth, the caravans' voyages? Who detects countries and regions, histories and stories, massed like a miracle in this city of ours? Who, these days, knows the true merchant of textiles? Who knows what we are? People come in, they buy, and within minutes they leave. They converse only to haggle over prices. It is no longer even necessary to place chairs around the vestibule of the shop. We no longer have any need for little tables on which to rest cups of coffee, glasses of tea, and ashtrays.

Diolen requires no conversation, demands no time. It needs no courteous company, no familiarity or adjustment. It is in a hurry, and it has no wish to escort those whose desires take them far. When Diolen came to the city, brides began to leave their trousseaus behind, stuffed in the wooden chests of their country grandmothers. They preferred to forget the embarrassing folklore of it all, those old garments and subdued colors and oppressive embroidery. So embarrassing—and all that is remembered of it now are the robes of shiny atlas and the crêpe paper that the *dabke* dancers on national television wear . . . .

Only the doll that continues to lie on the country bride's bed in her new formica-floored bedroom still wears the old fabrics, garments sewn by hand. Even the priest prefers quick Sunday vestments of Diolen over the endless chatter of his wife in the company of the old girls of the Congregation of the Immaculate Conception. If only the Armenian girls had not refused to do their embroidery on chasubles of Diolen, then he would have happily performed mass without all of those old vestments and relationships.

But isn't poverty a cause of it, Papa?

How can poverty be the cause when this country of ours never was as wealthy as it is today? Don't you see how the offices of foreign firms are mushrooming in the city center? Never have we had such lively prosperity.

No, son—we are at the threshold of a new and different era. We are on the threshold of an age of illusion, dictating that everyone must have access to all. Now, when a poor customer enters this shop she believes she has the authority of a veritable lady. She thinks that in moving through the streets and shops as her whims take her she has more freedom than she had before. But the age of Diolen—as you see—bound women's employment more closely to cloth precisely when its value plummeted and everything became fashion, impulse, *nouveauté*. I have already told you how such labels made it possible to sell anything anywhere, merely for the sake of selling and accumulating profit, completely isolating commerce from everyday life.

When you see women walking through the streets and souqs, moving amongst the crowds, have you been able to single out the odor of the woman in polyester, in Diolen? Have you seen the fabric of her skin? Have you noticed how a woman wearing nylon underwear carries herself, how she walks and speaks? Go one day to the Nuriye Souq, or to Souq Sursock, and see how the Egyptian merchant women buy mountains of those types of clothes for girls who sold their jewelry over there in Egypt, sold all they had in return for this new capital that will inflame the imagination of Arab Gulf tourists and the seasonal merchants from Upper Egypt. Can you imagine what smell the beds in those rooms give off?

New, odious smells, and new skin diseases that come with new fabrics. Eczema, dermatitis, spreading pustules and festering ulcerations, surreptitiously oozing beneath the electricity of the threads. Then an acid perspiration, a sour stickiness. Secretions of the base multitude, forced into close proximity.

That's the commerce of today's markets. The sun is setting on the age of the textile merchant. And it is not just the end of the merchant who trades in cloth, of course, but also the end of the art of tailoring and sewing. Madame Rahme knows perfectly well that now, mass bodies have only mass sizes. Now, she knows, it is a question of mass taste and *nouveauté*.

That is also the story of this city's homes. Look at the drapery, summer curtains, upholstery on chairs, bedspreads and sheets, handkerchiefs. Every one a flimsy weave that does not last, cannot be passed down. Volatile fabrics that leave no trace or impact, like the folklore on national television.

So it is the end, Papa?

No. It is the end of people like me, folks of my generation. We know that now we do not have enough time left to learn what will come next, to let tomorrow play in our imaginations. And so we are sentenced to a sweet nostalgia for what used to be, condemned to pondering regretfully the good things that are gone forever. No, it isn't the end of anything for someone of your age, because you will see enough to correct the mistakes and straighten out what has gone crooked. Nothing disappears quite like that, gone forever as it begins to decay. So do not listen to my exaggerations or my longings. Do not believe everything I say.

Nothing ends like that, utterly, in a puff of breeze, as it deteriorates. Didn't the inventor of the atomic bomb that annihilated hundreds of thousands in a single instant also invent carbon-14, the most reliable method to know the age of things, and to date the memory of the earth's insides? The clock in Hiroshima station, its hands suspended forever at 8:15 a.m.—isn't that the image that to the inventor will always signal the departure of the train of memory? And the photographic image, and then television—didn't human beings invent them when they realized that their faith had become shaky, diminished, and newly feeble?

What should I do, then, Papa?

Just look long and carefully at Diolen, and do not give in to forgetfulness.

I did not give in to forgetfulness, Papa.

I did everything I could, with all the means God gave me. I taught her what you taught me, and I taught her just as you taught me. And as it did for you, everything ended for me in suppressed sobbing, which I can release only now, and only in this land gone to waste. Only in this empty terrain.

Your father's words were of no help; his wisdom did me no good. What was it that we neglected to hear as we listened to his lesson, as we offered ourselves humbly to that legacy? Why did we extend our hands to cling to the cord that binds us to the generations, only to find the rope becoming a viper? How, when you loved me all that much and I was your only son, how could you hold out the viper's tail to me? What benefit is there if I tell my version now? How can I find a lesson in it when I have no offspring to take that lesson in turn, since I am the very last of the line, the severed end of the viper's tail, still coiling in the dust in vain?

I taught her what you taught me; and those things that you concealed from me I likewise kept from her. There was nothing I forgot to say. I don't think I made any errors or revealed anything that should have remained secret. But what does keep me awake at night are the torturous emotions of a lover abandoned for having committed an error that he cannot find in his accumulation of memories.

She abandoned me, Papa. She left me and went away.

Speaking availed me nothing. My stories were in vain. She reached the end before I did, and I became tiresome. All of me became tiresome—so tiresome that I had to be punished.

Good intentions do not suffice. To claim good intentions is not enough. They do not lessen the pain of the burning nor lighten the burden of regret that bears down on all the days to come, all of those remaining days on a mount so obtuse that, even if you're able to keep firm hold on its bridle, it will only take you with it along a path already fated and decreed.

Shamsa, who came to me at a time that had been set, has left me now.

My mother was asleep, the silk lay on the floor, and I was waiting for her. When she came in I begged her not to take off her clothes, not to wrap herself in the piled-up fabrics that lay undone before her. Look, I told her; and then listen, and only then, touch. If you take the silk to your body now, all of this will become inaccessible to you and it will be impossible for me to tell you its story as I ought.

How can you wrap your body so equably in what you believe is a fabric like any other? The most beautiful and precious, perhaps, but still a fabric, one textile among many that you know?

No, Shamsa. Silk is the only natural fiber on the face of the earth composed entirely of proteins. Wool is made up of cells, and cotton of cellulose—that is, the basic substance in the walls of plant cells.

The ways of silk making and even of silk's very source remained a secret closely guarded in the deepest Orient. The civilizations on the other side of the world learned its secret only at the end of the sixth century. Even Pliny the Wise wrote that silk is taken from down skimmed from the leaves of the cypress or terebinth tree, or from a worm that lives inside those trees. Hearing the story of silk before seeing it, Aristotle too—and the ancient Romans—believed it was gathered or made from the bark on the trunks of certain trees in a place they called the land of

Seres, a quasi-mythical country located according to Ptolemy somewhere near China, and according to Sanskrit writings in the country of Sirt, or the land of felicity.

Silk did not yield its secret easily. The affair demanded the cunning of the Emperor Justinian, overtaxed by Persian merchants' control over commercial markets. He formed an alliance with the Negus of Ethiopia, a fellow Christian, and they developed a joint strategy to be implemented with the craftiness of the monks. Two Nestorian monks made India their destination for the supposed purpose of converting adherents. There they perused the secret of silk. Upon their return, they explained the entire story to the ambitious emperor in all of its peculiar details. They made the voyage to India again, and this time they brought Justinian millions of silkworm eggs concealed inside two hollowed-out canes.

And so silk thread led caravans and ships, pulling in its wake philosophical and religious theories of being. With silk, India drew China and Tibet into Buddhism, and Alexander drew it as far as Greece, to canopy Rome after spreading across the Hellenistic lands and all of Asia. The Pax Romana guaranteed the spread of Christianity and silk together, and the Silk Road epitomized the many sorts of exchanges that occurred over a period of two thousand years from the moment of first contact between East and West, whether by land or sea. At the end of the last century we became one of the route's most important stops. For the sea route began at the China Sea, rounded India, plowed through open ocean to the Red Sea, passed through the Suez Canal and into the Mediterranean, and from there sailed on to Constantinople, Venice, and Genoa. The land routes passed through steppes and deserts, coming together at Tashkent and from there heading toward Baghdad, then Damascus and Beirut, and finally Constantinople . . . .

China's monopoly over the finest eggs did not last long, for disease struck the worms. And Japan was remote only until the Suez Canal opened. After that, quicker passage became possible: one could reckon the voyage as a number of days or at most a few months. However, through the year 1866 Japan did not permit the export of silkworm eggs through its closed ports. For some time before, many Lebanese towns had been suffering from a shortage of supply. Beirut, Tyre, and Sidon had become famous for supplying superior silk to Europe. The cities of Syria suffered as well, since most Syrian silk came from Lebanon, on average, two thousand tons.

Mtanios Khoury, a Beirut native known for his courage, decided to take things in hand. He traveled north to Turkey and from there to the Germanic countries. He caught a train to Vienna, to Budapest, and then journeyed on to Kiev and into the depths of Russia. On a horse that he chose with wisdom and care he crossed the Aral Mountains and entered Siberia, land of coldness. For forty days he traveled, reaching the Baikal Sea and following the bed of a river called the Amor to the Chinese border at the ocean's edge. There, Mtanios Khoury waited twenty days at the harbor of Sabirk. Finally there anchored a ship of the Dutch corsairs, which carried him—in exchange for a mound of gold—to Kabutiraya on Japan's western shore. And making his way from one district to another, Mtanios Khoury reached the city of Shikarawa that lay near—as he was told—a village famous for the quality of its silkworm eggs. How he came to an understanding with the village folk, how they allowed him to obtain the eggs, and how much he paid in return—all these affairs have remained mysterious, in spite of the many and various narratives told on his authority. And because of that man, a kilogram of Lebanese silk came to cost about sixty French francs. For a minimum of effort production flourished, for the Japanese cocoons were of such excellent quality that a mere six kilograms of cocoons yielded one kilogram of raw silk, while if the source was not Japanese, fourteen kilograms of cocoons were required to produce every kilogram of thread—and it was a silk of lesser beauty.

Before the Arabs carried silk to Spain and Sicily and taught the world how to dye it a palette of colors, it was the Syrian and Lebanese silk weavers who taught the technique of samite to the Persians and Chinese. For the weavers of the Levant had taken to fleeing to Persia, trying to avoid the harsh and restrictive surveillance of Byzantium. Their weaving traveled far beyond Byzantium and Persepolis, all the way to Ireland and the land of Flanders, and their brocades inspired the monks' art of manuscript illumination through the medium of Armenian and Jewish merchants. The influence of the Muslim silk weavers lived on in the decorative arts of Spain until the courts of the Inquisition imposed an age of blackness.

Many other things I told her, in endless detail. Then I said to her: Now. Now you can look.

Stop looking at me and turn your eyes to the silks I have brought you. Turn out the light, and leave only the glow from outside to come in on us, the light of the full moon and the reflections from nearby windows, illuminating the bareness of this room. Close your eyes for a few moments and then open them. Forget the glint coming toward you from the ceiling and corners: we'll return to that before long.

And now . . . we can hardly distinguish a particular color in our silks. So, what is it that we do see?

Everything you see comes from the thread itself, from the same two proteins, sericin and fibroin. That is what the specialists named them. But each fabric has its own special quality. It is like a pulse: common to all creatures, it varies slightly from one to the next.

How can we consider the difference—or the differences—between raw silk, the beginning, and the ultimate product, the fabric of brocade, setting aside the difference made by the gold and silver threads? Doesn't polished atlas, or satin, appear to be an entirely different textile than lampas or taffeta, though it is their nearest relation in the way the eye slips across their shiny slopes? And is gargan, which stands up as if by itself, really related to washah, pongee, surrah, tussah, and crêpe? The thread might be smooth or irregular; it might be twisted or polished with a stone that weighs tons. Some are made from leftover scraps of raw silk while others are worth their own weight in gold.

Only silk—unlike other woven cloth—requires long training, an apprenticeship in the look. Naturally, when we light up the room or carry our silks into the sunlight, things become easier—or so it may seem to us. An Iranian Sufi who always recited his prayers and the sacred names of God as he wove said that all fabrics are given color by means of dyes, and in hues that we choose and desire; but unlike all other woven fabrics, silk alone conveys the illusion of color. The light it reflects is mingled inseparably into its threads; it gives back that light in the dye we have chosen for it but the color is always tempered by the will of the thread itself. That is why the color of dyed silk never matches the original tone of the dye exactly. That is also why we see silk as a ripple of different colors that shift as our gazing eyes and bodies move.

The great Sufi Jalal al-Din al-Rumi says that in the rhythm of working with cloth lies that which organizes the universe. Were we to understand the great secret it enfolds, the very foundations of the cosmos would crack and all existence would sink into fatal chaos. It is the rhythm of woven silk, he says, the silken thread with its distinct echo, that might pull us nearer—if only illusorily—to this dangerous secret by compelling us to attempt its explanation. Thus, to handle silk and its sounds requires extreme caution.

Stay still, Shamsa. I will go over to the silks, and I will stir them one by one. Listen. Hear their voices, from huskiness to melodic chanting, from the far-off drum to the wailing of violins in the hands of blind lovers. And when I bunch some ends in my hands, when I imprison them and then let them go, what do you hear? Come a little nearer, and close your eyes so that their energy will pass into your ears. What do you hear? The sound of a pent-up brook suddenly freed, or a wave crashing onto hot sand, or the escape of a breath that trembles with desire, or the gurgle of milk in the breast before it streams into the infant's mouth, or the tremble of cold mercury across polished glass, or the whoosh of primal blood in the womb's lining . . . .

Are these the voices of things, or of live organs at the height of their activity? Is it the subdued movement of creatures of the shadow, inside a filament that is the thread and its own shadow, the image and its illusion in the mirror's emptiness?

I want to touch the silk now, said Shamsa. I want to wrap myself in it, to lie down naked within it, to surround myself with it. Then I will go on listening to its story. I want to be like a silkworm.

Shamsa's eyes held a gleam of desire that made me both wary and decisive. No, I said to her. Not right now.

Won't I spend the night here? she asked me.

No, Shamsa. Now you must go back to your home. You must linger for a while inside of what I have told you, what you have heard. Like the silkworm, you must fast a little, resisting the voracious appetite of your ears. Then, the story's spinning will reach its culmination.

hen Shamsa returned to me to hear the rest of the story, it was the last time we met.

She was in my mother's room when I came home. It was clear that she had arrived hours before the time we had set.

She was naked, wrapped only in transparent silks, layer after layer of different hues.

Hurriedly I stepped back, into the sitting room, my spirits plunging. I tried to repel the thoughts and images that chased each other into my mind, leaving it in crowded disarray.

The silks were piled up haphazardly and strewn about the corners of the room in a manner that confirmed my worst fears. But how had she known where they were, when I had hidden them so well . . . had my mother told her? How had my mother been able to guide her to their hiding place when she lay in her bed, unable to move?

I was so afraid that I found it hard to overcome my reluctance to examine the silks. My heart gave an enormous thump when I sniffed the lengths of fabric.

How could it have happened? How . . . and in what amount of time? As I questioned myself furiously, my vision went so blurry that I did not see Shamsa until she had come very near to where I sat.

I did not dare to look her in the eye. I did not dare to look her in the eye and I did not open my lips to let even a single word escape. In what amount of time, in what amount of time . . . . How many weeks have passed since our last encounter?

I did not dare to gaze at her eyes. Her belly was on a level with my eyes, and it was then that I suddenly became aware of how thin she had become. It scared me. Her entire body seemed to stretch sharply forever upward as if its past plumpness had evaporated in a matter of minutes . . . .

Without her fullness she appeared taller—snakelike, I thought, or perhaps she was a viper in the stooped silhouette of her body. Upright, she seemed to move not as a human being but rather as a sinuous viper.

Why have you gotten so thin, Shamsa? Are you fasting like the silkworm, as I instructed you to do last time? I said to her, making an effort to speak in an ordinary and humorous fashion that would put my sinister thoughts at a distance.

No, said Shamsa. I no longer need to weigh anything. I no longer need to feel that I stand solidly on firm ground. I no longer like to eat. I have found something better. I will become as light as what I am wearing. I might even try to fly. Like a butterfly.

I wanted to tell her that before it flies a butterfly must rip open its silk cocoon, must cut the filament. Everything that it has secreted throughout its life it must forget completely; when it becomes a butterfly, it must remember nothing about silk. To live the trivial, foolish, and rapidly fading life of butterflies, it must lay waste to its entire past. It must forget silk.

But before I could open my mouth Shamsa spoke again. Isn't it better to wear this than to die of suffocation?

Who knows, Shamsa? I answered her. Perhaps the worm is transformed into its own silk when it dies inside the cocoon. Perhaps it finds that life sufficient, there in the very meaning of its life.

But Shamsa was not listening to what I said. She gazed at me with eyes that had gone vacant, resembling so finely those of my mother. How much she looked like my mother now, in this thinness of hers . . . .

How can I try now—and why should I try—to separate seduction from the pull of nothingness . . . from death? Don't I know so intimately, and so profoundly, what the outcome will be and that it cannot be a successful or happy ending?

How, I wonder, how can I keep up with my longing to return her to me, when I know intimately and profoundly that Shamsa will not let me touch her, will not permit even a single caress, and that if I persist in wanting to sleep with her I will face the worst possible retribution and pain? For the crowning touch of Shamsa's beauty is not only that she keeps herself from me forever, but even more, that she stands poised to fly away, and I am so profoundly and intimately certain of her flight.

Do I name her coming illness a devastation, or is it the ultimate attainment of evil, the perfection of vice? Is it a crossing into another world that bridges the forbidden, a world that doctors call hysteria?

The sheen of her face stretched across her bones had a waxy reddish glaze, like old, tarnished gold. Her eyes, circling vacantly in their sockets, were not the familiar honey color that I loved, but rather sent out a greenish, bilious glow. Her mouth, usually a crimson tint that I could always visualize without looking at her, was now the purplish color of a blood-filled bruise.

My God, how beautiful and frightening was Shamsa! Could the world possibly hold anything more beautiful than this woman, naked beneath the fabrics that enveloped her? And could anything in the world summon terror more than she could? Whenever her heart pulsed with its rapid beat, I heard the silk shawls draped over her body rustle exactly at the point where they met her nipples. As Shamsa stood absolutely still, I heard the effervescent voice of the silk burbling deep inside like the sizzle of molten lead plunging into cold water. Now my head flamed with the fever of it, as in my boyhood, those times as a child when I was made ill by the evil eye of envy. Then, there had been wise practitioners who recited incantations for me; but now, where was the one who would help me to suppress this fever? Who would release this enormous appetite of mine, blocked as if by the words of an ancient talisman, immovable and able only to convulse and tremble in place—to shiver within the curse that held it fast.

Should I rest my hand against her hip, or would I give in to the fever . . . to that delirium that afflicted me as a child? I cling fiercely to my father's face so that I will see my mother rather than Shamsa. So that the attachments of incest will distance me from the fever of desire, and carry me instead into the fever of illness.

The raving of my fevered state rescued me from the vision of what I saw. I hurled away the image that tormented me, so like a demonic murmur, by assuring myself that it was the delirium's fault. I did not see what I just saw, I told myself, it just appeared that way to me, in my sickness-induced delirium.

My mother used to say, over and over: He sees only what he wants to see, he sees only what he wants to see . . . and by saying it she saved me. I really did begin to see only what I wanted to see as I automatically looked away from the source of the voice, from wherever a voice called me. It is how she kept me from giving away her secret to my father, as she addressed her sister but with words meant for my father's ear. He sees only what he wants to see. It is the habit of the blind, not of those who are shy.

My illness helped me and so did my love for my father. In my compassion for him I saw myself entering his body, my little body slipping quickly and easily into his. Why does she betray us, father? I repeated in my head, awake the whole night. Why does she betray us, when we love her so? The question pressed strongly and insistently against my head until it seemed to move inexorably through the repeated swings of a clock pendulum, as happens to people who have lost their minds and, cut off from the sounds of the everyday world, move to their own rhythms, withdrawing into a well of emptiness whose depth is unfathomable.

Bearing those enormous bouquets to her as we returned home from the shop in the evenings, to placate her irritation about our tarrying in the souq, I could feel the roses' thorns and the pointy stems of the big flowers pierce my hands and arms. I offered this agony of mine as penance, along with the sufferings of our lord Christ, as the priests had taught us. He who suffered, who was crucified, and who died for my sake, to absolve my sins.

Peeking out of the corner of my eye at my father's ever-jovial expression, I would ask myself in burning pain what our sins could possibly be. I would try so hard to imagine some sin—of mine, of his—that we had committed unknowingly, unintentionally, and perhaps had forgotten. But I could never locate anything. Perhaps, I would say to myself, perhaps my father was profiting a little more than necessary from his commerce. Maybe his cloth business was a little too successful. Perhaps he was committing the sin of self-importance, of arrogance, whenever he showed his pride in his father and in his vast knowledge of the seas of fabric and the histories of cities.

My father would ask me if what I carried was too heavy, for he would gladly take it from me. Hurriedly I would press the branches to my chest and say no. I offered my suffering as penance, with the suffering of our lord Christ, lifting my head from the branches toward the black sky, offering my vow to become a monk if only my father would not discover the secret.

As we climbed the stairs I would ask my father if our neighbor Sarah was pretty: did long, red hair make a woman beautiful? Laughing, my father would say he did not know, and my mother was the most beautiful woman in the entire universe. Seeing my troubled expression, he would add that I could not possibly understand just what a beautiful woman my mother was, because she was my own mother. And my aunt? I would ask him. Isn't my aunt a pretty woman? Yes, he would respond, but even though there is a clear resemblance between your mother and your aunt, your mother's beauty is a rare thing and you should be proud of it. Then I would all but say to him: And you—you can't possibly understand either, because she is your own wife. But with a rueful feeling I would pull back from saying it as I thought about the fragrance of the sweet carob and curcuma cake that always wafted from my aunt's open arms as she laughed when I did not understand her Egyptian Arabic.

He singled her out from among all the other women, and he fell in love with her. Thinking her the most beautiful woman in the world, he never ceased to find excuses for her behavior, and so what could I possibly do? He would open the door and usher me in ahead of him. We would find her seated in a nook of the sitting room, not yet having exchanged her street clothes for house garments, her mind straying far. My father would switch on the light, offer his evening greeting, and then give me a look, urging me forward with a jerk of his head. For the second time I would slip into his much larger body; running to her with my pretty bouquet, I would give her a hug. Together we would apologize for staying late in the souq, but she never passed up an opportunity to give us a tongue-lashing. She never accepted apologies. She did not put the bouquet in a vase.

She goes into her room to change clothes. My father carries the vase into the kitchen to fill it with water, and I run to my room and close the door. I do not want to hear the litany of his excuses, his low entreaties. I do not want to watch him adding salt to his food whenever she adds it to her plate as we sit at the supper table. I do not want to see her mouth chewing, humming a song, or kissing me. I do not want to see her mouth in the moustaches of Professor Kevork. I want to believe that the image of it is only a creation of my feverish delirium. But she gives me no help.

Yet I know that I saw what I saw. I was napping in the soft linen of the couch in Professor Kevork's sitting room, opposite the light in the corner that illuminates my mother's lower half as she stands next to the piano. It is as if her high, appealing voice in its repeated phrases is singing me a lullaby, lulling me in my nap, and so when silence comes I awake.

I knew immediately that I was not supposed to see. And so I closed my eyes hastily and I waited long before opening them. Did I wait so that they would finish what they were doing or so that I could make sure that I was really awake, that I had truly emerged from the illusions of sleep, from the specters of dreams?

Under the light from that corner her lips were on Professor Kevork's mouth. He was perched on his tiny seat in front of the piano and she was bent over him, her mouth over his and her hand on his shoulder. Their bodies were apart; she was not embracing him nor was he holding her. It was as if she were saying goodbye to him, in the manner that she said goodbye to her ordinary friends, except that her mouth . . . . It was as if her lips had slipped unconsciously onto his mouth . . . or I wonder, in the rapid glance that my eyes snatched, had I preserved only this one still image, extracted from their movements? From their kiss. From their embrace.

When we went out into the daylight I did not look at her. I put out my hand to hers and as usual she held it. I left my fingers there for the moments that felt necessary to imprint the smell of her hand on mine. And when I sniffed my fingers surreptitiously, the fragrance from Professor Kevork's shaving cream filled my nostrils, the perfume of the Old Spice in that white bottle that she had given him the previous Christmas and which my father did not like and refused to use. He preferred the large, translucent yellow bottle of al-Amaturi eau de toilette that so looked like piss. Its liquid looks so much like piss, father, and one day I am going to break that bottle . . . the white bottle of Old Spice that I rushed to the moment we got home, rushed to, and poured onto my cheeks and hands before my father returned from the shop . . . that way, he would believe that the smell on her hands and lips had come from me.

In the night I awoke from the fever, awash in my delirium.

She does not love me, Jirjis, said Professor Kevork to my father. She does not love anyone. She no longer loves anyone or anything. I was using the music and singing lessons as a means to hold on to her—and to give her something to hold onto.

I don't want to hear it, Kevork—

Wait, said Professor Kevork, interrupting my father. We must talk about it. I hope we can come up with a solution.

There is no solution now, Kevork. The matter is closed.

I heard the click of the key in the lock of the glass door that opened into the shop, and then I heard the brisk footsteps of Professor Kevork. I felt a pain shoot through my arm: my head must have been pressing down on it for a long time, dozing atop fabric swatches as if I were still a young boy napping on top of my schoolwork. I stayed where I was, not rising to join the two of them. For in spite of the passage of years since that kiss, or the delirium in which I had imagined it, I did not like the sight of Professor Kevork or whatever was connected to him. I did not want to see anything that had anything to do with him.

Just listen to what I am going to tell you, Jirjis. Listen to what I really was able to accomplish. I think there are aspects to this that you do not know, despite all of your learning. It is not a vice, Jirjis. It is an illness.

I know it is an illness, said my father, but it is an incurable one. A curse.

There is a doctor, Jirjis, a famous French physician, Dr. Gaëtan Gatian du Clérambault. By coincidence my uncle Vartan mentioned him to me. During the war, in 1916, my uncle met him in Greek Salonica. The man was ill. My uncle Vartan carried him off the road, where he had fallen in a faint, and took him to the French hospital. That's how they got to know each other. He had come down with malarial fever, and he also suffered from the effects of a deep shoulder wound. He had been hit by a bomb fragment during a reconnaissance mission behind German lines. This physician loved photography. He showed my uncle many photographs that he had taken in North Africa, where he was sent to recuperate after being hit and before going to Salonica . . . . In Morocco, Clérambault learned literary Arabic, and the Moroccan dialect too, so that he could talk to the local people. He wanted to learn whether what he had discovered in his own country existed in their land as well. He would strike up conversations by talking about the pictures he was taking, which had as their theme the local female costume and indigenous fabrics. For, seven years before he went to Morocco, this doctor had published a study entitled "Women's pathological erotic infatuation with fabrics."

At first glance, my uncle Vartan believed that this man was mentally ill, perhaps as a result of the malarial fever. That is what he told me, in any case. But they became friends and corresponded for years, for my uncle was—and still is—enthralled by that illness and by the stories of that French physician's exertions.

After the war ended, when my Uncle Vartan came to Beirut to live near us, he recounted to me how Dr. Clérambault went to Morocco, specifically to Fez, after leaving Salonica. He intended to come to Syria, and to visit Beirut, but he went blind in the aftermath of one unsuccessful cataract operation after another. When news of him no longer came, my uncle wrote to him at the Parisian hospital whose address he had used, to ask what had happened to him. Late in 1934, Uncle Vartan received a letter saying that Clérambault had committed suicide, shooting himself with his army revolver in his home in one of the Paris suburbs.

Why are you telling me all of this, Kevork?

To convince you that it is a true story and that I have checked it all, even if Uncle Vartan himself had suspicions about this doctor's mental state after receiving the news of his suicide. If the man had been right in the head, my uncle asserted, surely he would not have committed suicide . . . and perhaps everything he told me was made up out of thin air by his sick brain. For, does it make any sense that women would be infatuated with textiles? We've never heard of that in our lives . . . .

With silk, Kevork, said my father. Only silk.

Yes, only silk, Jirjis, but she is not alone in this.

I know that, said my father.

Just hear me out, Jirjis. I did not come to tell you what you already know. And I came to you only after obtaining a copy of this doctor's study by way of my sister's daughter, a dentistry student in Paris. These women all show parallel developments in their illness, and since there are so many of them it may be that doctors have started to follow their cases, studying their condition. Maybe there is a cure.

If you knew, Kevork, what silk is, then you wouldn't even hope for a cure, said my father.

But it is connected somehow to kleptomania. I brought her all sorts of silk swatches, but that was no good. What the study says is correct, and perhaps the first step is to treat the desire to steal, who knows? Before she steals silk, a woman with a condition like Athena's gets a sharp cramping in her abdomen, at once agonizing and pleasurable, and always out of her control. Her eyes become glazed with a layer of pain—it is pain and pleasure together when she sees silk, a great robe of silk, but she craves just a little piece of it. She isn't strong enough to rip it apart, though.

She doesn't have the strength to rip silk because she hears its scream

. . . all of these women speak about the cry of silk, and none can bear it. Haven't you noticed that for some time Athena's hands have been reddened, scarred, swollen? In the end, she did not succeed in taking the edge of the gown; she wanted to tear it herself, yet she could not endure it. She was crying in pain; she did not know how to tear it, as if she had lost the use of her fingers. She cried, shrieked—she did not want me to help her. They do hear the cry of the silk, its voices, when they finger and hold it, even when they approach it, as if they do not understand what it is, as if it is not fabric made of thread . . . .

But it is not fabric, Kevork. It is the only filament that we do not fabricate, that is born complete, perfect, pure, offered up exactly as it is, emerging from pure, living protein that does not die. We do not make it; we do not extract it, neither spinning it nor pulling it from plant fibers.

162

But they do not *fancy* silk, says Kevork. For example, they refuse to sleep in silk bed sheets or under a silk coverlet. And then, they refuse adamantly to wear it. You know that from Athena, but they are all like that. They consider that to sleep in silk or to wear it is an immoral act of seduction that they associate with prostitutes who use their bodies and beds to tempt men. So, Jirjis, it is not a vice. It is an illness that only strikes women and it is nothing like our illnesses—men's illnesses, our sexual diseases, I mean. It bears no resemblance to them at all. We might become attached to velvet or to fur, but it is a completely different matter since the only urge we feel for velvet or fur is to see it on a woman's body or when it conjures a woman's body in our imaginations. But what the study says, and now we know the truth of it, is that these women do not connect our images with silk when they make love to it. Its feel, its voices, its cry—none of them has anything to do with us, our bodies, our organs. They forget us completely; they no longer want us. We are not there in their desires. Nothing remains but the silk, the torment of their pleasure in it, the enjoyment of that torment, isolated from all other feelings. They give themselves up entirely to it, drawn to it as something beyond their will. They see nothing else. Clérambault's book says that the silk merchants understood silk's dangers and so forbade women to sell it. In an earlier time they locked up all the women employed in making it, in the weaving or the dying of it, and they let them out only for their work shifts. Years later, these women would be carried to the asylum.

Athena has not gone fully mad yet, Jirjis. She goes into a state of delirium; she invents for herself lives and roles. Perhaps she is trying to escape this destiny that she appears to recognize. She is not trying to torment us. She does not hate us. She simply does not want us, she does not want anything from us, and we serve no need. Haven't you seen that often she tries to atone for the enjoyment she takes in our torment? She is not malicious, Jirjis; you know that as well as I do. You know that she does not isolate herself from us out of dislike. But when the appetite takes her she must be alone, in the dark, and have no trace of a male there in front of her.

The silk moth lays eggs only in the darkness, Kevork. All its male eggs go as food for birds. Only in darkness and moisture does the thread come off the suffocated corpse, when the water boils, before it is crushed between huge marble slabs to bring out its luster.

Professor Kevork broke in to my father's words. Do not talk like that, don't say such things, Jirjis. Maybe the doctors are still working on it, in France . . . I told my niece to write to me.

I stayed where I was, motionless as a rock, hardly breathing. Professor Kevork went out and my father once again locked the shop's glass door. He turned out the light and, below, I was plunged into darkness. Then I heard his stifled crying.

At that moment I had only one prayer for my Lord: that he not bring her flowers that evening.

But he went on bringing her flowers, and roses, whenever we stayed late in the shop. And after he died I carried on doing the same thing, even when I was not late to come home.

And so he took her roses after hearing the news of Professor Kevork's suicide. It happened a few months after that evening in which my father wept, his sobs unending but suppressed. When she learned the news my mother showed no sign of serious grief. She appeared to be sorry. She mused a bit. It was sad, she said, that God had taken Professor Kevork just days before the premiere. Now, and without delay, she would have to find another teacher. That would be difficult, she added.

Afterward, my father no longer made any attempt to prevent my mother from visiting him in the shop. He gave her complete access to the lower level, to visit it alone as she pleased. None of us would ever go down when she was there, no matter how badly circumstances in the shop warranted it. And each time after she left the shop my father went down the stairs alone. I was always careful to offer to straighten the fabrics after my mother's departure, so that he would not grow suspicious that I knew his secret. My biggest concern, though, was that she not go to any other shop. For that reason, I spent most of my time hovering at the entrance to our shop, going in and out. I would walk down the street, examining both sides minutely, and I paid frequent visits to Hajj Abu Abd al-Karim. There I drank tea, feigning my enjoyment of the company of Abd al-Karim and his friendship. For my most frequent apparition was that she might enter their shop. I must be there to head her off, and to escort her back to our store.

In those days I had no sympathy for my mother, and my heart had no room for the mercy in my father's more capacious heart—my father, whose passion for her seemed not to have cooled in the slightest throughout the whole of those years. Watching him as he gazed at her, I asked myself whether he had not become more infatuated over time. And it was certainly passion, not merely kindliness or pity.

Sometimes when we stood, my father and I, in the Cathedral of Mar Jirjis, I would ask his namesake and intercessor to forgive me the moments of weakness that pushed me, albeit rarely, to hope for her death. To Saint George I would say: Intercede for me with the Messiah, that he may never hear me in these feeble moments of mine.

Her visits to the shop became less frequent and I told myself that it was a question of time. With age, my mother's passion would weaken and lessen . . . and that would leave a few years for my father to live without fear, at least without the fear of her descending into the shop. And I helped her to create her fanciful roles, her changing narratives about herself and us, so that she could cross over into that world of the imagination peacefully and reside there, in the illusion of that world and its sweet lightness.

As patient as a saint throughout that time, did my father know all of this? Was he awaiting, expecting, that she would walk that path with me until she settled there and his heart could feel reassured? Until he could once again go about educating me into what his father and the passage of time had taught him?

But my father knew that we lived in an age other than that of his father, and he was not true to the very visions that held the grandfather for whom I was named. My father did not say to me: Do not marry that woman, and do not live in this country. For my father died before Shamsa entered our house. And we did not live in the country of his father's era. Or, I wonder, did I simply not have his strength? Was I a weaker soul than my father had been at my age, and as a consequence did he not go so far as to advise a course of action that I was incapable of following? Perhaps it was that my grandfather's words to my father, which remained simply a matter of fine rhetoric shaped into the metaphorical vessel of wisdom sayings that the generations inherit and pass on without finding their own truth in them, were embodied in my mother's story, and realized there. The whole story, its past and its present, was already passé. It was futile to try to benefit from the lessons of the grandfathers. The advice was too remote for the coming days, and we draw on the lessons of experience only when it is too late . . . .

Thus we did not benefit, he and I, from the wisdom of my grandfather—or from the wisdom of anyone. All we learned, he and I, seemed to come at the wrong time, despite all of our preparations and calculations. It passed across us as if we had the transparency of silk. We left no trace. My mother, and Shamsa after her, would depart for a place that we had anticipated. We knew they would set themselves toward that destination. Perhaps we alone, with our foreknowledge, could have prevented and preserved them.

Or, I wonder, did everything happen as it did precisely because of that . . . as if our presentiments carved a path to it all, as if they pulled all toward it?

and my father continued. Listen, Niqula. For a thing of beauty to attain plenitude requires the destruction of everything outside of itself.

And thus the life that inhabits the cocoon is stifled before it reaches fullness. By night the gods wail, demanding victims and burnt sacrifices so that prayers to them will be recited and so that the border between the heavens and earth will be reaffirmed; so that the water will be forced back to the confines of the shores and imprisoned behind the riverbanks.

And when the thread's strength is joined unto its solidity the seduction of power knots itself firmly in place and so do the ruses of cunning and pain. Perhaps that is why the ancients restricted the wearing of silk to kings and sultans and saints and forbade it to everyone else. This was not tyranny but rather a shield against the lust for power, the illusions of might and the corruption they whet in individual minds and in society; against the possibility that absolute categories might become muddled.

Justinian did not set out to seek alliance with the Negus of Ethiopia of his own accord. It was not Justinian who designed the scheme of the two Nestorian monks, stealing away the larvae's secret in hollow sticks. It was his wife Theodora, daughter of the bear-handler in the imperial circus. Theodora had worked as a dancer in the taverns and then the brothels of Byzantium before taking up the profession of prostitution. She was a woman of beauty and intelligence. With a cleverness fueled by her passion for power she was able to reach the emperor and to marry him. She ruled with him before ruling in his stead, while the wise Justinian—who gave his name to the sixth century—withdrew into his predilections for architecture and the law. Theodora was a sorcerer—that is what some of the books say about her. Her greed and passion for finery did not stop at the outer limits of the empire: thus she had to have silk. And Theodora had to summon all of her cunning for its sake. When the peaceable, mild-tempered Justinian was preparing to flee from the wrath of the down-trodden, the hungry, and the rebellious after they had burned the Church of Hagia Sophia—the pride of imperial architecture—and many other buildings, Theodora held him there. She promised to take charge of the matter as long as he would never want to know the cost. She summoned one of her lovers, General Belisarius, for whom she had purchased an army of mercenaries. Do not return to me unless you are clothed in my favorite color, she commanded him. That day the sun set on more than thirty thousand slain commoners, and the next day's sun rose to reveal the red empress promenading her coralline silks before the icon painters. The manufacturers and weavers of silk in our country had to wait until the ninth century to flee the choking surveillance of Theodora's laws. Three centuries passed, during which each day witnessed the production of a mere five centimeters of brocade stamped with the seal of the imperial official.

In all of the stories of silk you will find betrayal, evil, and abundant covetousness.

It was not simply the bounties of the Nile that Julius Caesar sought as he waged war against Cleopatra. For the army commanders had informed him in their reports that this queen possessed "fabrics made of the breeze." When Caesar returned to Rome with the chests of the defeated Cleopatra, Rome saw silk for the very first time. The city's senators hurried to warn Caesar that wearing these 'breezes' would be detrimental to the morals of the city: it would be the beginning of the end, the hazardous prelude to decline and decadence. And sure enough, later on the Senate and the senatorial residences, their wives and their concubines, found themselves ensnared in silken filaments, struggling uselessly in their gummy resin.

Rome drowned in its own silk, submerging itself ever deeper until it sank under barbarian siege. To loosen his hold, the audacious and bold Visigoth Alaric's primary demand was five thousand garments of crimson silk, in addition to gold and spices. Although they gave him all that he wanted it was not enough, for when he opened the chests of silk, that unbounded desire swept over him and he pierced Rome like a sword stabbing water.

The sacred books of the Jews warned against amalgams and prohibited the plowing of a field with a team composed of an ox and a mule. But this was not in fear of uniting what God had separated, honoring boundaries between species whose violation would signal malediction and the victory of evil and its folk. Rather, the sacred word aimed to avoid combining the respective perfections of two pure kinds, that is, two species brought to consummate perfection through a single passion.

The earliest Muslims understood as much, as soon as they saw the silk of the Persians and the Byzantines. *Haraam!* they said. It is forbidden, they proclaimed, to fuse two such perfect temptations, the summits of desire: the body of a woman and the fabric of silk. So passionate was their longing for that female body that its encasement in silk beyond the walls of home must be prohibited. It is forbidden, they said; for it yields a perilous cupidity. An awful torture, and a test too taxing for human endurance, for the human eye that sees the forbidden. A source of chaos in the streets that brooks no laws of mercy and compassion, takes no account of where the modest abilities of people to control the call of their desires end. Thus the multitudes of Crusader soldiers, the wearers of hemp and wool, saw no silk in the cities they entered—except in the princely courts. The army generals wrote their dispatches, announcing to their capitals, so chilled and remote, that in the East they had seen lights emanating from coffers. They described the emirs' thrones as more splendidly fiery than the sun in these countries, even though it was unblemished by clouds. And so, they said, they must press on, fighting the battles; those at home must pluck the very last rural farmer from his muddy plot of land to arm him with a sword. The ships laden with coffers that burst with bewitching suns would not float but on seas of blood through which they must row on their homeward route to Europe.

But through long and slowly passing eons, silk's discoverers managed to preserve themselves from its evils . . . in great measure, at least.

An ancient Chinese legend relates that in the beginning the worm that becomes a moth was a princess, murdered by her father's wife, jealous of her loveliness and filled with envy. Her killing, or her burial alive, transformed her into filaments or eggs. This filament, then, was not offered in peace or as the blessing of bounty, and as we approach it we must remember this. As expiation before the deed, recognition of an evil inherent in its discovery and production—and to repel the consequences of its temptation—the Chinese sowed the ancient silk road with sacred sketches offered up to the Buddha in more than nine hundred and ninety grottoes dotted along a distance of eight thousand kilometers. A merchant would stop at each shrine to offer his devotions and supplications.

The Taoist Chinese silk weavers revered a text entitled *The Book of Changes,* composed in the distant past, the seventh century before Christ. It comprised sixty-four secret linguistic orders, and only each wise Grand Master of the silk weavers' brotherhood learned how to read its ideograms. Each formula is composed of connected lines that represent the male principle and interrupted lines that signify the female principle. Each represents the Tao, the cosmic principle that orders the world—indeed, the entire universe. The loom's warp is the yang and its weft is the yin. The closeness of the weave and the decrees that govern it represent the measure of our relation to the world and a calculation of our place within it, balanced between past and future. And how can secrets of this import be given to anyone but the knowledgeable and the wise? How can we entrust to the ignorant, the irresponsible, or the fickle the weaving of a silk like polished atlas, for example? The weave structure of this silk must be carefully calculated according to the number of points where it is warped onto the loom—whatever type of loom it is— to repeat a pattern, structurally and visually, that is known as 'satanic squares.' Actually called 'magic squares,' their chessboard-like arrangement in black and white signals at once opposition and concord, and brings into harmony all of the contradictions: between femininity and masculinity, night and day, yang and yin. They become 'satanic' if they manifest any flaws, no matter how slight or innocent these may seem. Thus, any blurring of unambiguous boundaries, drawn strictly between the ultimate examples of two pure categories, brings ruin down upon the order of things in the world, and evil's curses prevail.

My father taught me many other things, bringing to a close my last lessons in silk . . . the lessons he imparted before his death, as if to free his conscience and uphold the obligatory formalities.

Father, who killed me?

Who killed me? For I did not die a natural death. That I know.

I did not eat any poisoned plants, nor did the dogs take me as their prey.

I died without sentience of my demise, without preparing myself to meet the angel of death. I knew as much from the upheavals of things around me, and from the way time passed without me.

Was it stray bullets that felled me, after I lost myself in the burning streets and crept between the piled-up barrels, out to the still, vacant space?

Or was I blown up by one of the landmines left by the soldiers who passed along the seashore one day, cursing and shouting in a language that I realized later was Hebrew?

Or, I wonder, did the armed men get me? Posted behind the barriers I reached trying to escape the dogs, they sprayed their shot along the wall after lining us up against it while telling us that they were assembling us to transport us to safety zones.

Or did the strafing from the enormous military vessel out to sea dismember me with flying metal or flame that I did not see as it dropped onto me?

Who killed me? For I did not die a natural death. I did not see death coming so that I would recognize it and be able to meet it.

When I woke up my arm was numb and painful. I must have been lying on it for quite a long time. I did not wake up to find Thalj next to me. He lay a few steps away. I did not find the amphora girl, at whom I had gone on staring until I fell asleep.

The underground depths glowed in an unnatural way; I could see the length of the corridor. Dumbfounded, I stood up and stared around myself. When I looked up, right above my head, I could tell that it was sunset. Even so, the remnants of daylight were reaching me easily, pouring over me as if they were compressed into an upright column of light.

With two leaps I came out of the hole.

I looked this way and that. I could not believe what I saw: level ground, empty, like an open palm of the hand. A horizontal expanse, leveled and paved over, its even surface unmarred by any stray objects or protrusions.

A smooth desert without the sand, its curved horizon falling into the languid darkness, its expanse uninterrupted by any rise as far as one could see.

Nothing. No rock, no vegetation, no beast pawing at the ground.

I wheeled around. Nothing. I walked forward a few steps and stopped, because I had lost all sense of direction.

The sea, I said. I must find the sea. If I cannot find the sea, then I am either dreaming or mad, raving mad.

In the distance, still water reflected a violet gleam, now that it had closed over the sun.

I will walk down toward the sea. From there I will try to see where I am, pinpoint my location. And from there I will figure out the direction the shop lies in, or I'll see some landmark, something to guide me, so I can reorient myself to go on.

I turned around, but behind me I did not find the hole out of which I had come. I began to walk across this vast paving, my eyes fixed on the water. I was not afraid. I was intent on the water. I would reach it; all I had to do was to walk in a straight line.

Then I saw a sea of empty chairs, arranged in lines that made up large squares, like block formations of infantry. In parallel lines, they all faced the shore.

I stopped abruptly, bewildered, my mouth hanging open. They numbered in the tens of thousands, perhaps. Tens of thousands of chairs, arranged and ready for occupants who would sit and observe the sea . . . just so, directly across from it?

I stepped forward and began to make my way through the chairs, going down toward the shore. Before reaching the water, I came upon a wooden stage. The enormous theater lights above were not on. I saw a very large poster, in the form of a postage stamp, bearing a likeness of the singer Fairouz.

Suddenly, one of the spotlights blazed. I raised my hands over my eyes to shield them from the intense light. It so dazzled me that I could not see for several long minutes.

They must be celebrating, I told myself. It was a grand concert, held in the midst of this lovely autumn.

But I did not see the singer or hear her lovely voice. And when I discovered that there was no one to be seen in the rows of seats, I chose a seat for myself and sat down to wait for the concert.

From time to time my dazzled eyes register a calm layer of water submerging this entire paved expanse, so that I can see the sky and the resplendent September moon reflected in it. The sight makes me want to get up out of my chair and run in all directions. To till it well.

Then I ask myself why I should want to return to that. Have I not spent my entire life tilling the water?

Isn't that what we always did, father?

Acknowledgments

My liveliest gratitude goes to the Centre National du Livre (CNL), in Paris, for the fellowship that permitted me to complete this novel.

I thank also all of the friends in Paris and Beirut for their help in recalling places that no longer exist, in particular Adnan, Zeinab, Brahim, Josephine, Roula, Arlette, Joseph, and Hassan. And the others . . . .

Hoda Barakat
April 1998

176

Modern Arabic Writing
from the American University in Cairo Press

Ibrahim Abdel Meguid *The Other Place* • *No One Sleeps in Alexandria*
Yahya Taher Abdullah *The Mountain of Green Tea*
Leila Abouzeid *The Last Chapter*
Salwa Bakr *The Wiles of Men*
Hoda Barakat *The Tiller of Waters*
Mourid Barghouti *I Saw Ramallah*
Mohamed El-Bisatie *Houses Behind the Trees* • *A Last Glass of Tea*
Fathy Ghanem *The Man Who Lost His Shadow*
Tawfiq al-Hakim *The Prison of Life*
Taha Hussein *A Man of Letters* • *The Sufferers* • *The Days*
Sonallah Ibrahim *Cairo: From Edge to Edge* • *Zaat*
Yusuf Idris *City of Love and Ashes*
Denys Johnson-Davies *The Naked Sky: Short Stories from the Arab World*
Said al-Kafrawi *The Hill of Gypsies*
Naguib Mahfouz *Adrift on the Nile*
Akhenaten, Dweller in Truth • *Arabian Nights and Days*
Autumn Quail • *The Beggar*
The Beginning and the End • *The Cairo Trilogy:*
Palace Walk • *Palace of Desire* • *Sugar Street*
Children of the Alley • *The Day the Leader Was Killed*
Echoes of an Autobiography • *The Harafish*
The Journey of Ibn Fattouma • *Midaq Alley* • *Miramar*
Naguib Mahfouz at Sidi Gaber • *Respected Sir* • *The Search*
The Thief and the Dogs • *The Time and the Place* • *Wedding Song*
Ahlam Mosteghanemi *Memory in the Flesh*
Abd al-Hakim Qasim *Rites of Assent*
Lenin El-Ramly *In Plain Arabic*
Rafik Schami *Damascus Nights*
Miral al-Tahawy *The Tent*
Fuad al-Takarli *The Long Way Back*
Latifa al-Zayyat *The Open Door*